JANU~

M000307266

DEAR MARY —

GOD IS AT
WORK IN YOUR
LIFE! MAY THY
BOOK CONTINUE TO
GUIDE DOWN YOUR
JOURNEY.
    YOU ARE THE KEY
        — Jerome

THE GAUNTLET:

Five Keys for Unlocking Success in Leadership

THE GAUNTLET:

Five Keys for Unlocking Success in Leadership

A Leadership Parable

by Jerome Fogel

foreword by Julian Lowe

RESOURCE *Publications* · Eugene, Oregon

THE GAUNTLET: FIVE KEYS FOR UNLOCKING SUCCESS IN LEADERSHIP
A Leadership Parable

Resource Publications
An Imprint of Wipf and Stock Publishers
199 W. 8th Ave., Suite 3
Eugene, OR 97401

www.wipfandstock.com

PAPERBACK ISBN: 978-1-5326-9513-1
HARDCOVER ISBN: 978-1-5326-9514-8
EBOOK ISBN: 978-1-5326-9515-5

Manufactured in the U.S.A.   OCTOBER 14, 2019

Contents

FOREWORD

If you are reading this sentence right now, one thing is obvious: you desire to be a better leader. I am also certain that this is either one of many books you have read on leadership or the first of many books on leadership that you will read. And so I would like to take this time to congratulate you! I am celebrating in advance the many incredible things that will happen in your life as a committed student of great leadership.

As a pastor at one of the most influential churches in Los Angeles, and maybe around the world, I know a thing or two about mining for gold across the pages of hundreds of leadership books. In addition to pastoring a megachurch, I'm the current team chaplain of the Los Angeles Clippers and the coach of my 6-year-old daughter's soccer team. While you may have your guesses about which of these jobs is the hardest (and I laugh thinking about it!), I can promise you that all of these jobs require me to constantly improve my leadership. I have said many times that studying leadership books might be the single most important discipline that has sharpened my gifts and accelerated me towards accomplishing the purpose I was born for, and so I say again, Congratulations!

As you mine for the gold on the pages of this particular book, I want you to know that Jerome Fogel mines for the gold in the hearts of people.

One of the reasons I am so excited about this book is because I have learned so much from its author—Jerome is a man who knows how to persevere through difficulties and how to overcome them.

I can identify with Jerome. As someone from a tough neighborhood in San Bernardino, CA, I never thought I would be a leader. My mother passed away tragically when I was only nineteen, and that set me on a journey of losing myself in my financial and career goals. After a while, the only thing that mattered to me was making money.

Back in the day, the old folks I knew had a saying: "All money isn't good money." I never understood that saying until I found myself one day with a full bank account and an empty heart. This led to spending habits, addictions, and choices that left me broke and living on a futon at a friend's house in the beginning of my thirties. I had to overcome that, and I believe this is the common thread woven through every leader's life: he or she must be able to overcome failure.

Jerome has been an example in my life on how to do that, and now he has written a book that will help you do the same! Interestingly, there are many books and films about the rise and fall of great leaders. So many leaders live their lives addicted to the rise and afraid of the fall. You will learn from this book the dangers of that mindset. But more importantly, you will learn from this book not to be addicted to the rise and afraid of the fall, because if you have ever seen a sunrise or a sunset, you know there is beauty in both. I have learned this principle and many others from Jerome Fogel.

So why this book? Why this book when, quite frankly, there are so many others you could read?

Let me answer you with a story. Recently, I lost my car keys just when I needed to be at an extremely important meeting. There I was, right in my driveway, with a car perfectly capable of getting me where I needed to go, but because I had lost my keys, the car was rendered completely ineffective. This book, through a stunning parable, talks about the five keys of leadership and a leader who has lost his keys! I had a great car that was ineffective because of lost keys. In the same way, even bright, talented leaders can become ineffective if they lose a sense of their purpose and direction.

I have to believe that if this book is in your hands, you are a great leader, but you might be afraid of failure. Just like the day of that meeting, when my search for my keys got me back on the road to the meeting, I truly believe your search for your leadership keys in this book will get you back on the road to redemption. Life and leadership have their challenges—some avoidable and some inevitable—and sometimes I wonder if I am only finding beauty in the sunset because of the expected sunrise about twelve hours later. What if, in failure, the only way you find beauty in your "sunset" is if you patiently prepare for and expect your personal sunrise? I want to encourage you to read this book as I have: read it as if you are preparing for something more, something greater than what you have lost or are afraid of losing. Because you will overcome.

It's time to search for and find your keys. God Bless.

—JULIAN LOWE
Lead Pastor at Oasis Church

Acknowledgements

My heart is filled with gratitude for many people, too numerous to mention. Here is a handful who had a particular part in this book:

To Drew Tilton, who provided invaluable advice to me and formatted the manuscript before sending it to Wipf and Stock. To the team at Wipf and Stock, who took a chance on a first-time author. Thank you, Matt Wimer, Daniel Lanning, and George Callihan for bringing the vision to life with skill and passion. You have been professional and supportive from start to finish.

To Oasis Church: my life has flourished because of your investment, support, and spiritual guidance. To Pastor Julian: thank you for gracing this book with your powerful and encouraging words; I am a better man and leader because of you.

To the professors of the Institute for Spiritual Formation at Talbot School of Theology: I could not have written this book without the foundation you have given me. Thank you, Dr. John Coe, Dr. Betsy Barber, Dr. Judy TenElshof, and Dr. Steve Porter for giving me a trellis to abide in the true vine. To Dr. Kyle Strobel: thank you for being a mentor and endlessly encouraging and resourcing me as a first-time author.

To my copyeditor Jessica Snell, who taught me invaluable lessons on the craft of writing. The book would not be what it is without you. To my sister Lana and Sarah Hirsch, women I admire

Acknowledgements

and respect, who painstakingly proofread the final version and provided vital corrections and insight.

To my parents, Al and Parvin, who always believed in me, even when I didn't have the same belief in myself. I admire the lives that you live and learn from your loving example. I honor you, and I love you both very much.

Finally, to my beautiful wife Sheri: thank you for your boundless support, love, joy, and prayer. Your perceptive insight helped bring the characters of the story to life. I am honored to be a student of your ability to communicate and lead with grace, truth, and passion. I continue to learn from you, and I am a far better husband, friend, and leader because of you. This book could not have been written until you came into my life. I love you deeply.

In gratitude,
Jerome

Prologue

This book you have before you was birthed out of my own transformational experience. In the beginning of 2018, I stayed at a retreat house for several days. As the busyness and demands of normal life faded away, I began to face what was within me, journaling about my insights as I went. I saw patterns in my life and leadership that alarmed me. Something began to flow into me as I spent that time alone—words and encouragement came to me, and I can only point to God as their source. I had the thought that if I was going through this, perhaps there were others that needed this same encouragement.

This book is not something I had planned to write, at least not initially. But during that retreat, a brief outline of a fictional story came to me, and when I returned, I began furiously working on it for the first three months of the year, inspired by author Jon Gordon, who completes a book every December. The beginning of the writing process was enthusiastic inspiration. The middle of the writing process was dogged determination. And the closing of this writing process has been introspective reflection, as my own soul and imagination have rounded out the pages before you.

If only a handful of leaders are helped by what I have written, then I consider myself to have been faithful to the task before me. It is to you that I write. I pray that you are strengthened and encouraged as you read these words before you.

—JEROME FOGEL
   Los Angeles, 2019

1

The Rising Star

Jason Irving was a leader on the rise. In one year, he had led a dramatic turnaround of National Fitness Corporation's (NFC) Region Eight. This was his first assignment as Chief Operating Officer, and despite his successes, many in the other regions thought it would be his last.

Region Eight had hired ten different leaders in the last twelve years. For some inexplicable reason, it had always seemed like all the dysfunction and toxicity of the company drained into this one region.

As leader of the notorious Region Eight, Jason certainly had his hands full.

NFC had started out as a small gym with a mission to improve the health of its local community, and it had grown into an international powerhouse. But Region Eight was marred by backbiting politics, a lack of resources, hidden agendas, turf wars, misalignment, and self-centeredness.

Yet Jason had systematically transformed the culture, gaining positive notice from headquarters, other regional leaders, and employees within the company. There was a buzz, the type that

Jason inwardly craved and thrived on. His region had had a historic year—highest revenue of any year in the last twelve years, even though they still trailed well behind the larger markets. Jason was not the least bit concerned with this disparity though. He was confident that profitability and growth were sure to follow. He was convinced it was a typical J-curve scenario: an unprofitable drop followed by a rapid rise of growth and profitability. Jason encouraged himself by visualizing the success to come after all the intense and relentless work of the last year.

Jason had started as a personal trainer with NFC ten years ago, right out of college, and then received his MBA while working full-time in management. Leading the region was his biggest test to date as a leader. And he was doing well. He was known as hard-working and compassionate. He could speak as easily with the president as he could with the cleaning crew on the gym floor.

He had grown up as the son of immigrant parents who had learned how to survive. Hard work was ingrained in his DNA. He could remember his parents coming home late from the multiple jobs they took in order to provide for the family. He saw their example and followed it, studying for hours upon hours, determined to make something of himself.

Hard work leads to the executive office, he thought. *It's only a matter of time before someone sees what I am doing and hands the keys to me. I always knew I would amount to something.*

As Jason was thinking about his success over the past year, daydreaming over the successes to come, and simultaneously peering over his long to-do list for the day, he heard a hard, recognizable knock on the door. There was only one person in the company who knocked like that: Bill Benton.

Bill was as fearless a leader as they came. He was known for making the difficult decisions that no other leaders wanted to make. He once fired a regional manager when he had a hunch that the manager was opening a competing company. He did not wait for Legal to sign off on the firing either. At first, his general counsel, Maria Nadal, was upset, but a few weeks later she learned that the manager had been siphoning company resources and had planned to take key employees with him. Had Bill left him in his role even three more weeks, it would have been devastating to the region. Bill had that kind of foresight, combined with powerful command and control.

Bill did not pull punches either, and he would tell you about anything troublesome that he saw within you. Nothing seemed to shake him. Jason and others saw him as a warrior within the company.

Jason opened the door, and saw Bill standing stiffly, his eyebrows furrowed. His peppered black-and-white hair was neatly cut, and he was wearing a newly-pressed, dark suit of Italian wool that seemed to hug his broad shoulders as if it had been tailored that morning.

"Jason, I need you right now. Please follow me," Bill said forcefully.

Jason rose up from his chair, put a pause on his daydreaming, and walked down the hall with Bill. Was this finally the promotion he'd been expecting? Maybe CEO Benton was about to announce his retirement. With his innovative style and strong track record, Jason considered himself a top candidate for CEO.

I won't be surprised if I'm in consideration for the CEO role given my region's full turnaround, Jason thought. *This seems about as good a time as any to recognize the work I've done.*

"Have a seat, Jason," Bill said as they came into his office.

Bill shut the door and then settled into a throne-like, yet comfortable, black leather chair. His desk was a deep, thick mahogany, rounded at the corners. Bill had exquisite taste. Jason admired and appreciated it—and hoped someday to imitate it. Bill's office had a 180-degree view of the city, and Jason gazed out over the cityscape, noticing how the fall trees were slowly shedding their leaves prior to winter.

"Jason, I have to tell you what you already know: you are a young, promising leader. I have had my eye on you for some time now. You've turned around your region—a region that no one else could seem to wrap their heads around. You've created some buzz. I like what I see with the culture you've created, but . . ."

Jason's heart began to sink.

"We need to go in a different direction. There are some things I am seeing in your leadership that concern me. Also, there are two types of people in this world, Jason: farmers . . . and hunters. Farmers nurture business that comes in, but hunters . . . well you can count on them to bring in the big game. You've done an excellent job turning things around in this region, but NFC is going to need a different kind of leader for what we're doing next—a leader with a hunter mentality. We are bringing in Tom Giles from Region Ten, who has that hunter mentality. He'll be taking over for you and become CEO-in-waiting. I'm sorry."

Jason was devastated. Humiliated. *What is he talking about? "Farmers and hunters?" I know all about that! I've hunted in the past, sure, but that's not what this region needed. It needed a culture change first. He doesn't have any idea what he's talking about.*

Jason had always wanted to see himself as a fearless leader, but right now, he couldn't deny that he was flooded with fear. His self-image was crumbling.

He thought about his wife: *How am I going to tell Shaunny?*

He thought about his reputation: *What are people going to think of me?*

He thought about his finances: *How are we going to pay the mortgage on our new home?*

He started to panic. *I will never get hired again. I am going to be the laughingstock of NFC. Once you lose a promotion, it's the kiss of death. It's all over.*

He managed to compose himself and say somewhat meekly and requisitely, "I understand. Thank you for the opportunity." Inside he was fuming. *This company does not appreciate the work I have put in or the type of leader I am. The highest revenue in the last ten years! And this is the thanks that I am getting. I couldn't care less what happens to this place. It's all going downhill anyway. If they don't keep someone like me, who are they going to keep?*

All these thoughts were feeding into Jason's fear of rejection. He remembered being picked on as a kid, being made fun of for the way his hair looked when his mom would cut it to save money, for the cheap clothes he wore. He remembered his failures in school, in sports, in relationships. He felt sharp pangs of his conscience. His heart began to leak the guilt and shame he was feeling, and he did his best to cover it up.

But it wasn't over.

"Jason," Bill continued, "I know this has been hard to hear, but it doesn't necessarily end here."

Jason tried to turn down the volume on his thoughts. He wanted to listen to what Bill had to say.

Bill said, "I'm not going to leave you empty-handed. We have invested in you. I have invested in you. I put in a call to my friend Nick and asked if he would be willing to provide some coaching for you."

Coaching? What am I going to do with coaching now? Who provides coaching to the person he's just fired? This guy is out of his mind, Jason thought.

Jason was feeling sharpness in his gut. His mind was swirling with painful emotions. He was having trouble understanding that this was *reality* he was experiencing. But amidst this pain and confusion, he faintly heard what Bill just said.

"Nick . . . Nick who?" Jason inquired.

"Nick Savant," Bill said. He stared into Jason's face, looking for the deer to wake up from the headlights.

"Nick Savant?" Jason said incredulously. It finally hit him. That was hard to believe. Nick was the retired CEO of Brisbing and was widely recognized as the greatest CEO in that company's history and of all CEOs in the last twenty-five years, worldwide. Under his watch, Brisbing had experienced unparalleled growth, and leaders on his executive team had become successful CEOs in numerous companies. He was a legend and one of the most fearless and respected leaders on the planet.

But Jason was so disheartened after his firing that he did not think himself worthy of the opportunity. He only wanted to clean out his desk as fast as he could and leave before anyone saw him.

"Frankly, Bill . . . I . . . I don't know what Nick would want with me at this point," Jason said.

"Jason—you weren't quite ready for your role here at our company, and maybe I'm partly to blame for throwing you into this position with all of its troubles, but I don't refer just anyone to Nick. Most people can't handle his intensity," Bill said, as he handed Jason a card with Nick's phone number. "He's expecting a call." It seemed like Bill was trying to encourage him.

Jason shook Bill's hand and attempted to keep his chin high. He went back to his office and cleaned out the pictures and awards from his desk. Then he spoke with HR to finalize the termination, which was effective immediately.

Jason, still shell-shocked, said a few goodbyes to his leadership team and then headed out to the parking lot. The door handle of his car felt like it weighed ten pounds. When he opened the door, he plopped down in the seat. He put his face in his hands and wept. He was completely and utterly humiliated. Once he was able, he started the drive home, wiping the tears from his face and trying to cover up as much of the evidence of his devastation as he could. Despite his efforts, he knew he still had lines on his forehead and red, puffy eyes.

As he walked in the door of his house, he was greeted by his wife and her characteristic bubbly personality.

"Honey, is that you?" Shaunny asked, running down from the bedroom to meet him. "Isn't it kind of early to be home for a Friday?" It was 6:00 p.m. He usually came home after 8:00 p.m.

As soon as she laid her eyes on him, her face fell. It was clear she knew that something was wrong. She was very perceptive, as she had grown up in a rough neighborhood in the south and had to lean on street smarts to survive. At the same time, she had a father who was very supportive, though he was often gone for long periods of time as a military officer. She instinctively connected with people and saw through them to their souls. Jason knew she loved his soul and that she believed in him.

"Jason . . . what happened?" Shaunny asked, looking at Jason's downcast expression. "Have you been . . . . crying?"

If she sounded like she didn't believe it, well, she had reason. Jason knew he had never cried in front of her. Embarrassment at her seeing his weakness added itself to the roiling churn of raw emotions swirling inside him.

"I got fired today," Jason responded flatly.

"Whaaat?"

"I got fired today. And I don't give a rip anymore. It's over," Jason said.

"But you just had such a great year . . . babe, I'm so sorry."

"It was a surprise," Jason admitted. "But then again . . . somewhere in the back of my mind, I think I knew something was off. Bill had been riding me for weeks about sales and profitability in the region, even though no one else in the last ten years did what I did." He couldn't keep the bitterness from his voice. "How am I being compared to regions that have been profitable and steady for years? It's not fair. We are not even close to being on even footing." Jason could feel himself getting angry and defensive.

"Babe, we are going to be okay," Shaunny attempted to reassure him.

"Well, I hope so. We only have two months of expenses saved up. This new house was a terrible idea. I don't know why I thought this *wasn't* going to all fall apart. I need to start looking for work." Jason's attitude accelerated to the negative quickly. "I need to be alone for a few minutes. Let me wrap my head around this."

With that, he went upstairs and took a shower, hoping the hot steam would relax him. But it was no good: he was overwhelmed with what had happened. The rest of the night he obsessively replayed his conversation with Bill in his mind. *Maybe the indicators I thought I was hitting weren't that important. Maybe I'm not the winner I think I am.* Even though he and Shaunny usually went out for dinner on Friday nights, and he should be anticipating the joy of sharing a meal together, Jason's appetite was crushed.

He and Shaunny had met four years ago in his MBA program orientation. She was always the life of the party, a social butterfly who nonetheless cared deeply for people, getting high marks for warmth and engagement in professional reviews, and making friends wherever she went.

As Jason was finishing up his shower, Shaunny came into the bathroom and said, "Babe, we don't have to go out. I can pick up some Remarkable Chicken for you." Remarkable Chicken was fast food—and Jason's favorite comfort food. He loved their fresh chicken sandwiches and incredible service. But he was in no mood to be out in public tonight.

"Can you get me a number one with a lemonade?" Jason asked.

"Of course. I'll be back soon." With that, Shaunny left the house.

In the meantime, Jason finished his shower, put on his robe, and sat down on the bed with his head in his hands. He then lay down on his back, staring at the ceiling until Shaunny came home with dinner. She came in not knowing what to expect. Jason did not say anything when they sat down for dinner, Jason still in his robe.

"Here's your food, Jason," Shaunny said gingerly, handing him the white paper bag with *Remarkable Chicken* written on it in bold red letters.

Jason nodded and began eating. Shaunny could tell his mind was spinning.

"Mine is really good. How's yours, Jason?" Shaunny asked, testing the waters of conversation.

"Good."

"So . . . that must have been some day you had . . ."

"It was a tough one."

"You know," said Shaunny carefully, "it doesn't change how I feel about you. I'm so proud of you, and I know everything is going to be okay."

"Thanks. Let's hope so," Jason replied.

"Jason, I'm here for you. What do you need from me?" Shaunny asked.

"Nothing. I just want to eat right now," Jason said, dipping steaming waffle fries in ketchup.

There is a long, cold season coming, and there is nothing I can do about it, Jason thought.

After dinner, he and Shaunny retired to bed, but Shaunny would not give up finding ways to get into Jason's world. Yet still, he would not let her in.

Shaunny said, "Babe, I love you. Don't shut me out."

"I'm not shutting *you* out. I'm shutting *the world* out right now," said Jason. "I just need to process this for a night so I can figure out what to do next."

"Well, I love you and am proud of the business you built for NFC. They don't know what they had. But I do," Shaunny encouraged again.

"Thanks, love. Unfortunately, you are not the one making the hiring decisions. The CEO with five years in the chair thinks otherwise. And now I'm out."

"I know, and I'm so sorry, Jason. I'm here with you. I'm here for you."

"I know, Shaunny, I know. Maybe I just need a good night's rest."

"Okay, Jason."

"Goodnight, baby," Jason said, turning out the lights, and rolling on his side . . . away from his wife.

2

The Falling Star

When Jason woke up the next day, he felt as if he had been hit by a freight train. His head was foggy; he had tossed and turned the entire night, sleeping intermittently. Anger, sadness, and a host of difficult emotions began to surface, and when he tried to process them, it didn't go well. There were places in his soul that he did not want to face. Failure brought out the low self-esteem, self-loathing, and self-absorption hiding behind his successes. He did not want to face those painful realities within himself, and in that desire for avoidance he found a whole new motivation not to lose the game he now found himself playing.

Jason was therefore determined to power through the next steps, attempting to push his emotions to the side. Even though the firing came as a surprise, he always kept his fishing pole in the water, so to speak. In the last couple of months, recruiters had been reaching out to him directly for CEO roles at other companies. And he had listened. So, while the truth was that he was jobless today, he was confident the next job was just around the corner.

It's going to be NFC's loss, he thought. *They don't know who they let slip through their organization. I'm not only going to get my next job, but I'm going to make more than what I made before, with more responsibility. They were fools for letting me go. Let me get to a competitor, just so I can pin NFC to the mat and wipe the floor with them.*

Jason had been a high school wrestler and loved to compete, but in his first year wrestling he lost many matches, as he'd been forced to wrestle at varsity level (the only team his school had) even though he was a freshman. It had been a humiliating experience for him. The next year, he wrestled with a determination and an edge to him, often garnering penalties from the referees because of his force. His coaches didn't mind though. He took the team all the way to the state championship.

He was determined to prove that NFC was wrong for letting him go, but first he needed to secure the new job to validate that argument. He made a list of the calls he was going to make. Paul Norman was on the top of that list, a recruiter with ties to a majority of the large corporations in the city. Jason called him first thing in the morning. Paul had reached out to Jason last month about several executive roles, and Jason was confident that he'd like at least one of them.

"I'm shocked NFC let you go. Let's get the process started. Do you have time today for a phone interview?" Paul asked.

"It's not like I have a schedule today," Jason joked.

"How about 1 p.m., then? I can have one of my team members call you," Paul said.

"Great, thank you. Let's do it."

See, look how fast this is going to happen for me, Jason thought. *This all happened for a reason. Yesterday will be in the rearview mirror, a blip on the screen.*

Jason was waiting by the phone at 12:50. The phone rang at 1:00 on the dot. It was Barbara Montes from Norman Wakefield Recruiters. It seemed like a customary interview for Jason—typical inquiries about past positions, salary expectations, and the like. After finishing the interview, Jason asked his closing interview question, "Is there anything that would prevent me from being your number one, top candidate for this position?"

"Jason, we have many great candidates for this position," Barbara said, sounding a bit annoyed. "So, I would say nothing on this call in particular, no."

Jason took her response to mean that there was stiff competition. He was likely part of obtaining a diverse candidate pool for the position and perhaps was not the targeted candidate they had in mind.

That's okay, he thought. *Even a .300 batter has hall-of-fame numbers. Time to keep swinging.* He checked his e-mail and saw that he now had a video interview with ALG Logistics for their CEO role lined up.

That energized him, as he enjoyed having multiple opportunities on the horizon. He began to forget about his past at NFC with his new focus on what was in front of him.

The interview, which was with the Board Chairperson of ALG Logistics, seemed to be going decently, until the Board Chair checked his watch about an hour of the way through. Jason didn't think that was a great sign, but he told himself to calm down and to just wait and see.

The next day, he received an e-mail from the Board Chair that they were moving on to another candidate but that they would circle back with Jason if there was interest. That was a polite way, Jason thought, of turning him down.

By the end of the week, he had not heard back from Paul, and he was feeling anxious to get things going. He was ready to hit the ground running—why couldn't he make anyone else see that?

The following week he sent an e-mail to Paul to check on status. Paul replied later that afternoon:

> Hi Jason,
>
> I am afraid I have some disappointing news regarding your candidacy for the CEO role at ALG Logistics. They have asked us to interview some other candidates. There were a lot of candidates for the position, and they chose to include only those with extensive executive experience, many with CEO experience and a few others with technology experience. They were bothered by your abrupt ending at NFC.

I am so sorry. Hopefully, we will have the opportunity to work together on another search in the near future.

Best regards,
Paul

Another rejection.

Jason was hit hard by this one. *They were bothered? Go ahead with the traditional candidates, and you will get traditional results,* Jason thought.

But he didn't let himself sit in his frustration. He knew he still had a few aces in the hole.

Journey Limited, a direct competitor to NFC, had reached out to him in the past for an interview. He had not been awarded that position, but he thought the interview had gone well. It had been with Giselle Martin, the Chief Human Resources Officer. He picked up the phone and gave her a call.

"Giselle, how are you? It's Jason."

"Jason?" Giselle responded, sounding unsure.

"Jason Irving. I interviewed about five years ago for a management role. Do you remember me?"

"Oh right, friends with Mark. What can I do for you?"

"Well, I want to let you know that I just became available. I finished up an assignment with NFC as COO. I'm currently interviewing, and I'm seeing if there's any interest again," Jason said with hope.

"Jason, I'm glad you called. We have an open COO role. Listen, I like you, so I'm going to tell you something off the record. Word got around of your availability, and I gave Bill a call to find out what happened. He told me that you aren't ready yet for this role. I can't tell you much more than that."

"Thanks, Giselle. I realize Bill has said this, but don't you think he's afraid of me going to a competitor? There's a conflict of interest here."

"I'm not sure he is afraid of anything anymore. Bill has been a straight shooter with me in the past, and there's no reason for this to change. But again, this is all off the record."

Jason was fuming inside, but he was not going to show it.

"Thanks for being frank with me, Giselle. I'm glad we spoke," Jason managed to say politely.

"Good luck, Jason. I'm sure you will find something."

I am going to destroy Bill and NFC now. This is personal, Jason thought.

There still was another ace in the hole, though it wasn't a direct competitor of NFC. Jason had e-mailed an old friend from college who knew a leadership coach named Jon Brames. Jason proposed running Jon's west coast office, a branch that did not even exist yet. That was the type of out-of-the-box thinking that Jason knew he brought to the table. He was hopeful he could arrange a meeting or call in the next couple of weeks.

In the meantime, Jason contacted everyone in his network and let them know he was available for executive opportunities. He sent out hundreds of e-mails and letters and went to several networking events. Nothing was coming up for him. One Monday morning, Jason checked his e-mail. It was Jon Brames.

> Jason,
>
> Good to hear from you, and great idea. If you are very serious, come to our leadership conference next year in May. That way we can meet in person. Make sure you hurry because seats fill up fast.
>
> Sincerely,
> Jon

Jason took this to mean Jon was intrigued, but not enough to begin conversations now, as the conference was nearly eight months away. Jason was devastated, as he did not have eight months to spare. There was only another month of savings left in the bank.

This was my last lifeline. It's already been a month, and now nothing is coming up for me? Maybe I need to go back to being a personal trainer. Maybe I'm not cut out for being an executive.

Jason spent the next two months in a haze. He read the news obsessively, watched television for hours, ate glazed donuts by the dozen, and avoided people who knew him from NFC—anything to keep his mind off not finding a lead, nor having a job. He would look out the window at the trees, now without leaves and barren.

His haze was broken, eventually, by Shaunny, who asked, "Babe, what ever happened to that guy you were supposed to meet?"

"What guy? It doesn't matter. I'm in winter. This is a season of death. Things have to die," Jason said morbidly.

"You know, that CEO . . ." Shaunny hinted.

"What are you talking about?" Jason asked angrily.

"That number Bill gave you. Remember?"

"Oh, you mean Nick Savant?" It had completely slipped Jason's mind. *I'm desperate at this point. I will do anything,* Jason thought.

"You know what?" Jason was beginning to be inspired again. "I will call Nick tomorrow. It's a long shot, but we have one week left before our mortgage will go into default anyway."

And I'm not going to let that one week go to waste.

3

The Invitation

Jason had a palpable sense of excitement that seemed to burn away the haze he had been in for weeks. He was beginning to feel energized again. He dialed Nick at 8:30 a.m., but there was no answer, so Jason left a voicemail.

"Uh . . . hi, Mr. Savant, this is Jason Irving," Jason said, his voice beginning to crack. His hand shook as he held the phone, and Jason tried to keep it under control. "Bill Benton gave me your contact information a few months back and told me to call you. I'm sorry it has taken so long. Please give me a call when you get this. Thank you, and I look forward to speaking with you."

He hung up the phone, and he could hear the silence. He peered out the window again. He saw the trees, barren. His eyes followed one tree down to where it met the earth, to where its thick roots drove beneath the surface and gripped the soil. Then the phone rang.

It had only been two minutes, and it was, indeed, Nick Savant.

"Jason, great to hear from you. I didn't recognize the number, and I still screen my calls. But this is important. Bill told me all about you." Then Nick got right down to business. "Listen, I do not have much time, but can you be here tomorrow?"

"Um, yes," Jason said. *I can't believe this is really happening.*

"For a few days, actually. I need you to stay with me for a few days. More like a week. Then you can be on your way."

"Sure," Jason said. *I better jump on this opportunity now before he changes his mind, or talks to Bill, who might sabotage me.*

"My assistant Brian will reach out to you with all of the details," Nick said.

"Excellent, thank you!"

"Jason. This is going to be a great week. Stay positive," Nick encouraged.

"Uh . . . okay." Jason found himself at a loss for words. He had just been on the phone with *Nick Savant,* perhaps the greatest leader of his generation.

And "positive" was not something he'd felt in a long time.

He hung up the phone and leapt with his feet in the air like he was jumping over a lineman tackling him at the knees.

He instinctively then called his wife. "Shaunny!" Jason yelled into the phone. "You won't believe it! Nick Savant just invited me to *his* place this week!"

"Wow, I was wondering why you were calling so early. Babe, I am so excited for you! So . . . do you know what you're going to wear?"

That was typical, Jason thought, suppressing the desire to laugh. He was thinking about this leadership opportunity, and Shaunny was thinking about fashion. He loved how she approached life so differently than he did.

"What? No, I haven't really thought about that. I guess I'll bring a range of stuff—a suit, casual attire, and everything in between. I want to be ready to handle any situation I find myself in."

"We need to go shopping!" Shaunny said firmly with delight. Jason knew she always wanted him to look good. She always believed in him and thought he deserved the best.

"I don't want to spend the money. We're days away from defaulting on the house. Maybe a shirt. But not much." Jason was worried about their finances. Even though Shaunny was working full-time for a nonprofit, they'd built their budget around two incomes. He needed to start working again and had even put applications in at local department stores. He did not tell Shaunny this, though.

The next morning, Jason was packed and ready to go. He even had a new custom-fitted, pinstriped cotton dress shirt that Shaunny had picked out for him. When they were first married, he hated that she would try to impose her style, but he had grown to appreciate her more and more as the years went by. She saw the value in him, and she wanted the way he dressed to reflect his worth.

He had also spoken with Nick's assistant Brian the day before and received specific instructions. They were . . . odd. Jason was puzzled and a little intimidated by not knowing exactly what he was getting into. But surely someone like Nick Savant knew what he was doing.

Jason gave Shaunny a gentle kiss goodbye and left their house. She always seemed to want him to keep kissing her forever. He gave her two seconds. He was anxious to be on his way.

It's a relief to leave all of this, Jason thought. *I'm going stir-crazy here at home every day.*

He followed the directions Brian gave him, driving north along the coast for about an hour.

It is so good to finally get away. I can't believe how hard this has been for me. I thought the transition was going to go so much smoother. And rejection after rejection. I don't know how much more of that I could have taken. And then there's the financial pressure. This is hard, and I don't fault myself for applying to department stores. I need to provide.

As he was driving along the coast, the sun was just beginning its ascent into the sky, mostly hidden behind the clouds. But he could see several slivers of light breaking through. They were highlighting the ocean in bright, thick lines, then bouncing off the water and flashing in his eyes. As he pulled up to the address he'd entered into his navigation, he saw tall, ivy-covered walls on both sides of the drive, hiding the house. In front was a guard gate with security personnel, handguns at their sides. As he came to a stop, a large, muscular gentleman with a trimmed mustache and aviator sunglasses leaned over and looked in his car.

"Your name, sir?"

"Irving, Jason Irving."

"Identification please."

The security officer took Jason's ID and looked intently at him, and then he brought the ID with him into the office, scanning it. He then nodded his head and came back to the car.

"Okay, Mr. Irving, you have a good day. Wait until the gates open. Then go ahead and go up the drive." The road he pointed to was gravel-covered and winding. "You can park in one of the two spots next to the guesthouse at the end of the road." He pointed ahead of Jason to the side of the mansion coming into view as the gates were opening.

"Thank you."

"My pleasure. Enjoy your stay."

The gates had fully swung open. A view was opened to a sprawling beach mansion made of stones, large enough that it could have had a moat around it and it would not have been out of place. There were white marble fountains, and the ocean was visible again, waves sparkling in the sun.

As Jason came to the end of the driveway, he could feel the muscles in his shoulders begin to loosen. He located the spots in the corner that the security guard had alerted him to and pulled into the one on the right.

This place is amazing. Wow. This is like something out of a movie.

He then looked down at the instructions Brian had sent him.

Jason, please enter the guesthouse through the side gate that says "Welcome." Once you go through that gate, you can pick up the keys waiting for you on the white marble table.

Jason exited his car and took his luggage from the trunk, then wheeled it out with him through the gate. He gazed upon the two-story guesthouse, which was attached to the mansion. There were two entry doors next to each other on the bottom floor. He spotted the marble table just inside the gate and located the keys.

He noticed that the key ring had five keys on it. *Okay, which key do I use? Which door do I take?*

He tried the door furthest from him with each key, but none of them opened it. He was not sure which door was his. *Am I supposed to go into the main house?*

He then frantically tried to place the keys in the first door, which seemed to be attached to the main house.

The fourth key worked. He finally managed to open the door. Once he stepped inside, he found himself in the guesthouse. The initial instructions from Brian told him to explore and delight in the space he was given for his stay. There were two floors, and they contained two bedrooms, a bathroom, a living room, a kitchen, and one extra room that seemed very peaceful.

This season since his firing was the first in many years when he had no leadership responsibilities. And now that he was at the Savant estate, he felt freed from worrying and thinking about his next position. It was indeed delightful to get away. He gathered the rest of his bags and brought them in.

Then Jason heard a knock at his door. But it wasn't Brian. It was Nick. Wearing a crisp polo shirt and tan pants, he had a strong, slender build with a mix of dark black and grey hair. He held two Remarkable Chicken bags. One for him, and one for Nick. Jason remembered that Brian had asked him to fill out a brief survey, which included a question about his favorite food.

"I like your taste in fast food," Nick said.

"Yes, it's my favorite, Mr. Savant." Jason smiled.

"This is what I call a power lunch," Nick said. "And call me Nick."

Jason shook his head. He was about to have a sit-down with Nick Savant, the five-time CEO of the year, according to Board Room Magazine. Even though his emotions told him he couldn't believe it, in his mind it was beginning to sink in.

And Jason couldn't acknowledge that reality without holding it together with this one: the last time he'd had Remarkable Chicken, he had just been fired from NFC.

4

THE GAUNTLET

Jason was nervous, to say the least. He was enjoying his lunch but was having a difficult time in the conversation. Frankly, he was a little intimidated. *I was confident in my leadership abilities before I got fired,* Jason thought. *I would have gladly sat down with Nick a month ago, my head held high. But I was just pushed out of National Fitness. This is kind of embarrassing.*

"Thank you so much for having me here," Jason said in between bites. His mind was racing. "This is a very special place you have."

"My pleasure," said Nick. "You can accomplish a number of things over the phone, but getting to know someone is not one of them. Nothing beats sitting down with someone eyeball to eyeball. And over thousands of years and across all human cultures, sharing a meal has been a universal experience of intimacy. As for this setting, well, after my first six months as CEO of Brisbing, I found I needed a relaxing atmosphere to retreat to. My wife, Debbie, and I collaborated on this estate. The landscaping is hers, but the retreat feel is my contribution. I stitched it together from a number of experiences in my life. Enough about me, though," Nick concluded abruptly, leaving Jason to reflect that Nick seemed direct, but in a very self-aware way.

Nick continued by saying, "Now I'm going to shoot straight with you here. From what I heard, you have great potential, but why do you think Bill sent you here to me?"

Jason was taken aback but attempted to remain poised. He reflected a bit for an answer, then said, "I think Bill saw something in me that he liked enough to refer me to you but not enough to keep me at National Fitness."

"Well, it's certainly never easy being fired," Nick said, leaning back in the chair. "Let me tell you, I was fired from two jobs for poor performance and nearly pushed out of three other companies."

He looked at Jason thoughtfully before adding, "And this is not technically a firing, but one of the memories seared into my consciousness was being passed over for a full-time offer after a summer consulting role in grad school. It may seem like something insignificant, but that was the first time a failure shook my self-confidence to its core. And I wanted so badly to be a winner."

Jason could understand that. Thinking something was in the bag and then . . . well, having that bag snatched out of your hand . . . he knew, from oh-so-recent experience, how that could shake a man to his core.

Nick continued, "All of the great leaders I know and have studied have experienced failure. Abraham Lincoln faced bankruptcy, lost elections, and was fired from more than a job or two. He failed many times over. Great football coaches have been fired from head coaching positions before they won a championship. Successful entrepreneurs have been fired from positions early in their careers, failed, and gone bankrupt before they made it big."

Nick paused, took a sip of his drink, and then continued, "What's my point, you might be thinking? Getting fired is painful, it's humiliating, but it can also lead to a turnaround. It can force you to look honestly at yourself, your heart, and your motives.

"It is also an excellent motivator. It wasn't until the last time I was fired that things changed. I would spend so much time blaming other people and things: my supervisors, my fellow employees, lack of training. And while much of what I saw was true—poor training, dysfunctional cultures, and a lack of servant leadership—what's more important is the truth I did not see: I was prideful, I did not dig deep enough when joining these companies, I was often motivated by greed, I was afraid of making mistakes, and I was unaware of what it took to be successful."

Jason was listening intently. It was rare to hear a leader share honestly about his failures with such excellent perspective. Jason was still hurt and upset with NFC. He was upset with Bill for firing him and for spreading a negative story to keep him from getting hired at Journey Limited. Jason felt like he could identify too much with the portrait Nick painted of his greedy, fearful younger self.

Jason said, "I never knew those things about you. All I've ever read about you has been about your success as a leader."

"Jason—what I am about to say, you have to think about, and you have to think about it hard. *What makes a successful leader, and what are the keys to being a successful leader?*"

Jason answered quickly. "It's about results and exceeding goals. You have the record for training the greatest number of leaders who have gone on to be CEOs, the record for the greatest number of profitable quarters, and the most awards. *You* are successful."

Nick looked at Jason silently, and eventually Jason found himself dropping his gaze. It was like Nick could see right through him: like Nick could see right through his flattering words to his childish desire to gain Nick's favor and approval.

Nick said, "Those are the *results*. But what are the *keys*, what are the levers that produce those results? You see, it wasn't always this way for me. I battled through failures for much of my life. I had great leaders in my life in different areas, and I learned a great deal from them, but ultimately I had to go on my own journey to discover those keys. And so do you. By the way, do you have them with you?"

"What do you mean?" Jason asked.

"The keys. Do you have them with you?"

The keys from the table? Nick was moving from metaphor to concrete reality so fast that it made Jason dizzy. "Yes," Jason said, "I have them here in my pocket. Honestly, I wasn't sure what these keys were for."

"Ah. Now that is why you are here. During your stay, you are going to learn the keys to what makes a successful leader. I can tell you this: it's not going to be easy. I'm going to challenge you. I'm going to push you towards and past your limits. It's going to take everything you have, and then some, but I promise you that you will never be the same leader again—ever. Are you up for it?" Nick was looking at Jason with that calm, unflustered stare again. It felt like he was looking deep into who Jason was at the core. Like he was calling Jason out from who he was, to who he was going to become.

Jason was nervous but excited. "Yes, I am. Count me in."

Nick continued, "Jason, your mission for the rest of your stay here is to discover the significance of those keys. You have the rest of today to yourself. Your mission begins tomorrow morning when you wake up. So, get some rest."

"I will," Jason said. And then, because Nick looked at him like he was still expecting something more, Jason added, "I promise you, I am up for this, Nick."

For the first time in a long time, Jason was looking forward to the challenge in front of him.

5

THE KEYS

Jason spent much of the night thinking about his conversation with Nick and looking at the keys in his hand. He also passed by a note on the kitchen table at the guesthouse that read:

> Welcome to the Leadership Gauntlet. We have thought
> of everything that you could possibly need. There is also
> a guidebook to the property in the armoire if you have
> any more questions. Please contact my assistant Brian for
> anything further.
> —Nick

After reading through the note, Jason only wanted a good night's rest. He was weary. And he had one, which was much needed. Jason woke up the next morning with a sense of palpable excitement. He was waiting for instructions on what to do next. By 9:00 a.m., when he had not heard anything, he reached out to Brian via a phone on the property.

"Jason, good morning. How can I help you?" Brian said when he answered.

"It's going great, Brian. I am so grateful to be here. Nick mentioned yesterday that we would get started in the morning. He did not mention a time, but I thought that 9:00 a.m. was early enough to check in."

"Jason, thanks for checking in with me. The mission has already begun."

"Wait—what?" Jason asked, confused.

"The mission has already begun. That's all I can tell you," Brian said.

Jason tried to compose himself, but he was upset to learn that he was already falling behind, "Okay, so am I on my own on this mission? Are there any clues? How does this work?"

"All I can tell you is that you need to figure out why you are here and why you have those keys in your hand," Brian answered.

Jason took the keys out of his pocket and looked at them again, with more intent. There were five keys of differing shapes, but nothing seemed to stand out to him. They looked like ordinary keys. Nothing that was likely to open a treasure box or anything else exotic. Jason was even more confused but was determined to get to the bottom of this.

"Okay, let me think about this, Brian. Maybe I'm missing something. I will get back to you if I need anything."

"Very well, Jason."

Jason hung up the phone and sat down on the large recliner in his room downstairs. He started retreading the conversation in his mind and pondering what the keys could mean. He was at a loss, until . . .

He remembered the note he'd seen the night before, mentioning a guidebook to the property. The first day he had explored the space, but he had never looked at the guidebook. So, he darted upstairs to the armoire.

It was an older, rustic armoire that smelled like fresh lemon polish. When he opened the door, he saw a binder inside, as well as thank-you cards from various leaders around the globe. Some of the names were senators, coaches of professional football teams, current CEOs of major corporations, and pastors. It was a *Who's Who* of leadership.

He then reached for the binder and pulled it out, closing the armoire. He gathered himself together and sat down on the tufted, leather couch in the living room. He opened the binder and the first page read:

> Welcome to the Leadership Gauntlet.
>
> This retreat space has been designed to renew leaders and bring into focus their mission in life. Everything here on the property is for you to explore and delight in. Here in this binder, you will find, among other things, a history and map of the property. Two of the keys provide access to space in this property. Of those two, the larger bronze key opens up the first door downstairs and the back door. The other three keys provide access to three other properties in this city. Each key opens a space which contains within it a specific leadership challenge. When you complete one challenge, you will move on to the next one.

Jason remembered how he had ignored the instructions on the day before. That was like most of life for him. He often forged his own path, sometimes stubbornly in the wrong direction. It worked well sometimes, but other times it caused a lot of trouble.

Okay, now where do these keys provide access?

He began walking through the upstairs hallway and noticed the door that seemed to lead into the main house. When he had first arrived, he was sure that door was not for him. But now he grasped his keys in a move that was part inspiration and part desperation. He began trying each one.

"Nope, that's not it," he concluded as he tried the first key.

He moved to the next key.

"It's not this one either."

He moved to another key.

"Nope again."

He tried the fourth key.

"Not it."

Finally, looking at the last key, he slipped it in the lock. And then—he turned it open.

The door opened directly into another bedroom. Inside was Nick, tending to a young man sitting in a wheelchair. Jason was startled to see them there.

"You made it," Nick said to Jason as if expecting him. "You are behind schedule, though. I want to introduce you to my son, Mark."

"Nice to meet you," said Jason.

"Ni-i-i-i-ce to meeeeet . . ." Mark paused and shook uncontrollably, then concluded, "y-ouu."

"I want you to hang out with Mark today, okay?" Nick said to Jason. Then Nick turned back to his son and admonished him, with a twinkle in his eye, "And, Mark, you be nice to Jason now!"

"Dad, I'll," Mark said, "try not to maaaake . . . thissss . . . one cry!"

Nick laughed and Jason forced himself to smile as he thought, *What have I gotten myself into this time?*

6

Joy Journey Foundation

"Get used to Mark's humor," Nick instructed Jason. "He was born with cerebral palsy, so he has impaired motor function that has become progressively worse over his life, but he is as sharp as they come. So stay on your toes. He may shake uncontrollably at times and need some basic care, but for the most part he is independent, maybe even a little stubborn, like his dad."

Just then Brian walked in. "You guys ready? Let's go."

Leaving Nick behind, Jason and Mark followed Brian through the main house. As he walked, Jason saw an oil painting that was ten feet by ten feet, with bright yellow streaks and a depiction of blackened buildings. He looked at another painting of a tree, blossoming in springtime. The colors were vibrant, and as he looked at the paintings, he could see the artists' signatures on the canvases in slightly-raised dark ink. These were originals, alright.

They exited through the main door to a van parked out front. After helping Mark into his seat, Jason assisted Brian in strapping Mark's wheelchair to the inside of the van, the outside of which was marked "Joy Journey Foundation." Jason sat down in back with Mark.

As Brian started the van, Jason joked, "So are we going on a journey of joy?"

"No, not exactly. That's the name of the foundation Nick founded," Brian responded, as they exited the property through the front gate. Brian then began sharing more of the story.

"When Nick graduated from college, he took a bicycle trip across the United States that changed his life. Along the ride they would stop at different cities to raise funds and serve people with disabilities and their families. It made a lasting impression on him, but he did not think about it in terms of his own life until Mark was born. When Mark was diagnosed with cerebral palsy, Nick and Debbie began having trouble adjusting to their new life. And it was not necessarily a problem that money could solve.

"One day, Nick was in his office and feeling overwhelmed, when he looked up at a framed jersey on his wall. It was a jersey signed by all of his teammates from the ride. That inspired Nick to contact some of the founders of the ride to help him set up this foundation here in his city. They now serve children with disabilities and their families by providing a space for them to find their 'Joy Journey' as we call it."

"That's incredible." Jason was impressed but also it raised a legitimate question. "So there's joy in raising kids with disabilities?"

"There sure is. You will have to see the foundation's work—and find out for yourself what we mean by it. Speaking of, here we are." Brian had pulled to the front of the foundation's headquarters.

Jason and Brian opened the doors and stepped out of the van. Jason was careful to help Mark out of his seatbelt and onto the sidewalk.

They are going to see what kind of person I am, Jason thought. *See, I am helping Mark. I am a good person.*

Jason, after all, wanted to make a good impression on Nick, and he did not want anything negative getting back to Nick about today's challenge. He was still nagged by the suspicion that Bill would contact Nick as well, and he did not want to add any fuel to *that* fire. Still, Jason was puzzled as to what the challenge was exactly. In the meantime, he was beginning to see in Mark the go-getter independence that Nick had told him to look for.

"Jaaaa-son. Want to see me dive in the pool? Let's race to the deep end!" Mark began speeding towards the entrance and was soon lost in a sea of children crowding around him.

Jason darted after him, while careful not to inadvertently bump into any of the other kids. "Mark, please don't!" Jason laughed, as he caught up to him. "I don't think your dad would appreciate me pulling you out of the pool today."

Brian was unloading boxes out of the van. He called over to Jason, "I need your help setting up a couple of things. Today is a barbecue, with a puppet show and dance-off. I'll need your help with all of it."

Jason still wasn't sure what this was all about, but he was sure Nick was somehow watching, so he wanted to do his best.

"Sure," Jason said. "But what about watching Mark?"

"Don't worry, your job isn't to watch Mark. He's old enough to take care of himself here. It's getting him in and out that's the tricky part. But I do need your help setting up a couple of things. Can you man a grill?" Brian asked.

"I'm no chef, but I can hold my own." The truth was that Jason didn't think much of his own grilling skills, but he was going to help anyway.

Jason proceeded to barbecue for the two hundred people packed into the patio area. The space was equipped with touch-screens, audio commands, and accommodations for everything a person with a disability could need. While taking care of the grill, smoke was building up in Jason's eyes, but he was determined to get this right and ensure all of the meat would be cooked properly. No one was going to get food poisoning on his watch. Parents were coming to Jason with various requests: cheeseburgers, hot dogs, veggie patties, and chicken. He was happy to help. Meanwhile, he could hear the happy screams of children in the background. He saw them running around in circles, jumping in the pool, and running laps around the property playing tag. The line for food began to pile up. There were so many needs, and Jason could not seem to keep up. He was beginning to become stressed from the overload of requests. But he was not going to let anyone see that. He did not want Nick to see him stressed out under pressure.

When the lunch was over, and the kids and their parents had full stomachs, Jason proceeded to clean the grill and burn the remaining residue off it. During that time, he found a few moments to wolf down a cheeseburger and a hot dog for himself. He was already tired.

But they were just getting started.

When the grill cleaning was complete, Brian, seeming to appear out of nowhere, handed Jason a script.

"What's this?"

"This is for the puppet show," Brian said. "But it's not just any puppet show. You will be playing a blind boy named Cesar. Read through the script. You have about ten minutes until showtime."

Jason began feverishly studying the script, and Brian began giving him pointers. *Ten minutes, why so little time?* Jason wondered. *I am being set up for failure.*

"Get a feel for the characters and get a sense for the flow of the story," said Brian. "I don't expect you to get this word for word, and I will be doing it with you, so if you get stuck, I can help you along."

When Jason took to the platform to give the show after the ten minutes were up, he was somewhat terrified. He had always struggled with performance anxiety, and in this leadership challenge, he did not want to fail. So at first he was anxious, but as the show went on he began to have more fun. The show was about two boys, where one boy (Rick) meets another boy (Cesar) who explains to him what it's like to be blind. And they become friends.

As the play progressed, Jason found that he loved hearing the laughs and sounds of the children in the audience—and the less he thought about his own performance, the better he could hear them.

He finished to roaring applause from the crowd.

Jason turned to Brian. "Brian, that was fun, but I'm glad that's over."

"Perfect. But can you dance?" Brian responded.

"What!"

"We are having a dance contest. Don't worry, you're not in the contest. It's for the kids. But it helps when you dance with them—they enjoy having adults be silly with them. Go out and have fun."

Fun was not likely. Jason did not like to dance one bit. But, to his surprise, as he started to reluctantly obey Brian's instructions, he discovered he enjoyed seeing all these kids with different disabilities—cerebral palsy like Mark, and also blindness, deafness, Down syndrome, and paraplegia—let loose on the dance floor. There were children of all ages out there. To see them dance nearly brought tears to his eyes. Many of them were dancing with their parents or with each other. Despite their disabilities, he saw many smiles among the sea of children, parents, and volunteers. Jason decided to help a little girl named Maria dance. She was all smiles in her motorized wheelchair, turning and twisting. And Jason was right there with her.

After thirty minutes, Jason heard Mark's voice over the loudspeaker, making an announcement. "We have a winner. Annnnddd the wi-i-i-inner is . . . Maria!"

The crowd broke out into applause, Mark and Jason included. Maria's face lit up with a smile.

At that moment, Nick walked in. The crowd of parents and children erupted in applause and cheers once more. And Mark wheeled up beside him.

Nick then began to speak, and the crowd became very quiet.

"It was over thirty years ago that I cycled across the country for the Joy Journey fundraiser. I was just a young, wide-eyed college kid, much too full of myself. But something changed in my life during that trip. A seed was planted. I saw the lives of children with disabilities and their families changed.

"Here is the story of the day that changed me: I had just finished a long bike ride on a hot day; it could not have been less than 110°. I was exhausted. I was so thankful *that* day's ride had ended. When we arrived, there were parents and their children with disabilities ready to welcome and greet us. As I dismounted from the bike, I said to one of my teammates, 'I'm so glad that's over. I hope

I never have to ride in this heat again.' A little boy overheard me; he could not have been more than six years old. He was a paraplegic. He came up beside me, tugged on my jersey with his little hand, and said, 'I wish I could ride a bike.'

"That hit me. I had such a poor attitude, and I had lost gratitude for the joy in the journey I was on. And here was this boy who could only wish that he could ride a bike in the heat, sweating, and with his legs burning like I was. And that is what this foundation is about. Helping you and other families find the joy in the journey that you are on."

Then he put his hand on Mark's shoulder and said, "And you have this troublemaker to thank for the Joy Journey Foundation. And one more thing. Let's thank Brian for coordinating today's activities, and also thank Jason who, I heard, cooked well on the barbecue and played a great hand puppet. As for his dancing, well . . . he's about as good as me." Everyone laughed, even Jason.

Then Nick walked off the stage and waved Jason over.

"How's it going?" Nick asked.

"Hi, Nick. I'm tired. But in a good way. Something was different about today."

Nick nodded. "When you focus on serving the needs of other people, you forget about yourself."

Jason felt encouraged, like Nick thought he was getting it. "I haven't thought this little of myself in weeks. In weeks, Nick."

Nick replied, "I know it. I did something like this for over sixty days one summer. I wasn't mature enough to fully appreciate it, but it was a crash course in leadership through service. Jason, do you have that keychain with you?"

Jason reached into his pocket for the keychain and showed it to Nick.

"Look at that first key, Jason, and remember that the first key of leadership is service. As a leader, you have been appointed to serve other people. That is the first thing I check when I'm assessing a leader. That concept runs through the organization, no matter what the organization is. It runs through the financial statements, the corporate offices, the strategic plans, through the employees and to the customers. This holds true for CEOs, senators, coaches, spiritual leaders, you name it. I check who the leader is serving—himself or others. The truth is that I have done both, and I have had both types of leaders over me. I began to thrive when I had someone over me serving me, and I bet you have too. That is the first key. *The only type of leadership is servant leadership.*"

Nick paused and then challenged Jason with a question: "Who were you serving at NFC, really?"

Jason was tired, but he understood what Nick was saying. It made sense even from his own life experience. He realized that he had begun serving himself at NFC. He wanted to be noticed. He wanted big things to happen. He wanted to be seen, known, and honored for being great. He even felt a bit ashamed, remembering that that very morning, when helping Mark, all he had thought about was what a good person that made him—about how good *he* looked, and not about the person he was supposed to be serving.

"I wanted to make a big splash. I wanted to be noticed. I wanted to be known for being a great leader. I wanted to be a CEO more than I wanted to serve others," Jason said.

Putting his hand on Jason's shoulder, Nick encouraged him, "That's good, that's good. You are beginning to have self-awareness. Your motives are hidden beneath the surface. They are what's driving you. If you are not careful, they will derail you. The jump from the leadership team to being the leader is a treacherous one, not for the faint of heart. If you want the position to meet your own needs, you will be leading out of a deficit, rather than leading to serve and overflow in love to others. In my mind, this unresolved problem is what I see most in leaders today. I know it's not realistic to expect that our hearts will be completely pure when we serve, but the first step is to be self-aware and to know what's driving you.

"Let's get you back home. You have another big day tomorrow."

Jason had a lot on his mind as he helped Mark back into the van and headed back to the Leadership Gauntlet. But it was hard to think through any of it well because he was so exhausted.

After this first day of the Gauntlet, all he wanted to do was sleep.

7

The Optometrist

Jason woke up the next morning tired but energized. He was
ready to serve more. He was inspired by what Nick had done for
those children and families. He jumped out of bed and picked up
his keys. At 7:30 a.m., a much earlier start time than the day before,
he looked at the set of keys and compared them with the other
doors that connected to the main house.

As he was about to attempt to open another door, he heard a
knock at the front.

When he opened the door, it was Brian.

"You ready, Jason?" Brian asked.

"Yesterday was a great day. I'm energized!"

"Good to hear. Follow me."

They got into Brian's sedan and headed out of the gate.

Jason couldn't contain his excitement. He had been in a long
season without movement and accomplishment, and now things
were finally happening. "I'm ready to use this key. What's next?"
Jason asked.

"I'm taking you to see Dr. Morris."

"Who? Is there something wrong?"

"Nothing is wrong," Brian said, smiling. "It's for a checkup."

Fear began to grip Jason. He did not like going to the doctor, especially one he did not know. *What if they catch something? What if they find something wrong?* But Jason didn't want to let Brian in on his internal dialogue.

Brian then pulled up to Costmart. "Okay, here we are."

"Costmart?" Jason said. "There are no doctors here."

"There's an optometrist here. It's the only one Nick goes to," Brian responded.

Brian walked in with Jason to the optometrist's office just inside the store's wide front doors. The receptionist asked Jason, "How can I help you?"

She then caught herself, seeing that Jason was with Brian. "Ah—you must be Jason Irving. We have you scheduled for 8 a.m. Please fill out this paperwork and have a seat."

As Jason was filling out his health history, he was mostly wondering where all of this was headed. *Why am I at an optometrist's office? This makes no sense.*

Once Jason completed the paperwork, the receptionist looked it over and said to him, "Okay, Jason, I see here that you wear contacts, correct? Please remove them for the eye exam. Here is a lens case and contact solution for you."

"I will, but I warn you, I will not be able to see anything," Jason joked. He figured that if he had no idea why he was there, he would roll with it and start having some fun.

Jason removed his lenses and then sat down for a series of eye tests, checking different aspects of his eye health. The one he hated the most was the one that shot pressurized air into his eyes.

Dr. Morris then came into the waiting area and greeted Brian. "Brian, good to see you. How have you been? How is Nick doing?"

"I'm taking care of things for Nick today. He's super-busy but he is very happy right now, because super-busy is how he likes it," Brian said.

"That doesn't surprise me," Dr. Morris said.

"And I'm doing great, especially since it's not me getting my eyeballs blasted with that air!" Brian said.

"Funny you should mention that. This is our last week testing intraocular pressure that way. We have a new test coming in a few days. We have to track and implement innovations in optometry, or we'll get left behind." Then he looked at Jason. "You must be Jason."

"Yes, sir," Jason said.

"Come, follow me."

As Jason stood up and started following him, he joked, "I can't see you, just so you know."

"Don't worry, you aren't missing much!" Dr. Morris replied, without missing a beat.

Jason laughed. "That was a good one."

"Have a seat," Dr. Morris said. He started by asking him a series of mundane questions about his health, and then he said, "Now just relax. Try not to blink or squint. I'm going to put a machine over you that is going to test your distance vision. Don't try too hard. Let the vision come to you."

He performed a series of tests with lines of letters. He would ask, "What's more clear: this side, or this side?" Some of these were easy to distinguish, and others were more difficult.

"Now, we are looking for clarity when we make these comparisons," Dr. Morris said.

When he was done, he summarized, "Everything looks healthy. You have responsive eyes, good muscles, and there is no degeneration. We are going to give you a little stronger of a prescription, but other than that, you are good to go. Tell Nick I said hello."

"Thanks, doctor, I will." *I appreciate the prescription, but what am I doing here? Again, this makes no sense.*

The receptionist came back in and said, "Brian's ready for you outside."

When Jason left the doctor's office, Brian met him.

"You made it out alive!" Brian joked.

Jason played along with the joke by answering, "Barely!" But that felt dishonest, because he really was uncomfortable with his lack of understanding of what they were doing. Was honesty part of the whole *servant leadership* principle he was supposed to be operating on now? Maybe. So he decided to say what was really on his mind. "What is this all about, Brian? What's next?"

"We're going to WallLand," Brian said.

"WallLand? You can't be serious."

"I am. Follow me," Brian said, with a smile that seemed to be hiding something.

When they arrived at WallLand about twenty minutes later, Jason was struck by its size and excellence.

WallLand was famous for its innovation around the world. Its theme park covered 10,000 acres and welcomed over 1,000,000 guests each year. There was also a film, television, and product empire tied to and integrated with the park. Jason appreciated what type of leadership it took to run something this vast—and to run it this well.

As Jason entered, he was welcomed by the employees with smiles—real ones. The place had a palpable sense of positive energy about it. Brian and Jason were taken on a personal tour of the park on a golf cart—overviewing its history, features, and hidden details that weaved together a fantastical story. Michael Wall was a mysterious figure. He did not do interviews and was known as a reclusive genius. Jason was impressed and intrigued by all of WallLand in its intricate detail and perfection. Finally, near the end of the tour, the guide let Jason and Brian out of their golf cart and pronounced: "Jason this is our last stop on the WallLand tour."

They were directly in the center of the park, next to a tower forty stories high. It had floor-to-ceiling glass on each floor. There were sculptures of WallLand characters crafted in marble at the bottom. The lines of the building were precise, and the metal and stonework contained subtle but intricate patterns within them. Legend had it that the fortieth floor was where Michael Wall himself worked feverishly, often sleeping in his office, as he looked out on the park and its guests. Brian led the way for Jason, until they came to a sign that said, "Employees with security badges only beyond this point."

"Are you sure we're going the right way?" Jason asked.

"You're good, Jason. This is where I leave you," Brian replied.

Jason walked up to the sign, looking for how he would enter the tower. He noticed a red buzzer by the sign, just below it, with a speaker. When he pressed the button, a professional and energetic voice responded right away, "Can I help you?"

"Uh, yes, I'm Jason Irving."

"Mr. Irving, we were expecting you. Please swipe your security badge," she said.

"I'm sorry, miss, but I do not have a security badge," Jason responded.

"That must be incorrect. Mr. Savant surely provided you with one."

This is . . . well . . . weird. There are no badges here. I hope I didn't leave it in the guesthouse somewhere. All I have are keys.

"Give me one moment, please," Jason said. He took his keys out and began flipping through them. He noticed a faint symbol of WallLand engraved on one of the keys in his hand. *This must be another clue.*

"Miss, I do have a key though," Jason said.

"Then you do have your badge."

"I'm not sure you are following me. I have a key, engraved with a WallLand symbol. That's it. No badge," Jason said, frustrated.

"Mr. Irving, that is the key to your badge."

"I must be missing something here." Jason looked again at the key, seeing the engraved symbol, but this time he noticed now that it was a button. He pressed it, and the key split in half, swirling open to reveal a tiny guest security badge with Jason's name on it. The key, now in half, became a small clip that could be placed on his shirt. "Never mind, I have it now," Jason said. He swiped the barcode register next to the buzzer.

"Thank you, Mr. Irving."

Just then he heard a sharp buzz, and the door opened. He clipped the badge onto his shirt.

Jason then walked through the iron gate and into the building. He was amazed by a floor-to-ceiling mural in the distance, filled with the characters of WallLand. As he walked closer, he saw sculptures on the right side of the foyer. These traced the popular characters from inception to the present. To the left of the mural, there was a timeline that comprised pictures of Michael Wall, from one of him standing on the vacant land where the park would later be built, to when the park first opened, to the present day and the sprawling WallLand empire. Jason then approached the elevator, where he was greeted by a security guard who asked for his security badge. When Jason showed him the badge, the guard swiped it. He then escorted Jason to the elevator, where the guard pressed the button for the top floor for Jason.

Jason went up forty stories, to the top. As the elevator climbed up, he began to wonder, *What's next? And who will I meet next?* He heard a faint electronic bell ring, and the number forty appeared on the elevator monitor. The doors opened onto an expansive executive office space, where he was greeted by Nick . . . and Michael Wall himself.

"Jason, I want you to meet someone," Nick said.

Jason looked at Michael Wall. He was a dark, tall figure, with a faint mustache, dark hair, and a finely tailored light grey suit.

"Yes, hello, I'm Jason Irving. This has been a fantastic tour so far," Jason said, marveling at his experience. He couldn't believe he was meeting Michael Wall.

Jason kept looking directly at the man. This was a man who, while in his seventies, clearly was aged but full of energy. He then reached out his hand.

"Pleased to meet you, Jason. I'm Michael Wall. I am very glad that you enjoyed the tour. The reason this place exists is to elicit the reaction that you are giving now. It fuels my passion to see your wonder. Please, come have a seat."

Jason sat down with Michael on a tufted couch in cigar brown, next to his desk. Jason could see a 360-degree view of WallLand and the surrounding cities in the distance. The sky was lit up bright blue, and the clouds provided a touch of white.

Nick started the conversation, "Mike—you and I go back a few years, I would say."

Michael responded, "Yes, indeed, Nick. Here I was, on the verge of bankruptcy. I was completely focused on payroll for our employees and on paying my family's mortgage. I was gripped in fear. Someone from our Board recommended speaking with this hotshot leadership coach—someone younger than me. I thought to myself, 'It was my original artwork and last penny that jump-started this empire. What could I learn from someone ten years younger than me?' But I did. I picked up that phone and invited you over for coffee. I told you what I was afraid to admit—to anyone. I seemed to have completely lost vision for WallLand. Creditors were calling us incessantly. We were deciding which bill we were going to pay—the electricity, the water, the mortgage. It was the darkest and most despairing time of my life. And this kid—well he wasn't a kid at the time, he was thirty-nine years old—this kid takes me to the optometrist. I will never forget it. I was desperate at this point, so I went with him. And the optometrist said something to me I have never forgotten since."

He then turned to Jason. "Do you know what that is?"

Jason was hanging on every word that was coming out of Michael's mouth and was startled by that question. "Let me think," Jason said. "This day has been a whirlwind, and I'm not seeing the connection between the two, not yet at least."

Nick interjected, "You need to pay attention to everything that is happening. Leadership, companies, and lives can turn on one insight, one thought. That's all it takes."

Jason's mind raced. He began to picture Dr. Morris's face and glasses, replaying in his mind's eye the series of eye examinations. Then it seemed to come to Jason, and he said, with hesitance, "Let the vision come to you."

Michael exclaimed, "Yes . . . yes, Jason! Those words spoke in my ears as if it was Beethoven's Symphony No. 3 in E Flat Major. It then became so clear. I had no vision because I could not see—my fear and self-centeredness were blinding me. In the early days, my leadership team was drinking vision from a firehose—there was more of it than we had time for. But at this point in our history, I was a dried-up faucet that would not even give a drip. Not one drip!

"Well, after I'm finished with this optometrist, we get in Nick's car, and he begins a series of rapid-fire questions. He starts diagnosing me. It seemed as if he had me figured out and was simply confirming what he knew. I was staring right at my problems: the bills, the park in need of repairs, the leaders who left, my marriage problems, my health, the stress levels. I had completely lost sight of why I started WallLand in the first place.

"Then the light bulb goes off. Have you ever appreciated a gifted mechanic who, when you pull your car into his shop, determines the problem after listening for only a few milliseconds? Well, it was, I tell you, just that remarkable with Nick.

"He told me that most coaches are too afraid to tell their clients what they need to hear. They focus on strategy, people, plans, the latest theories, but really the problem starts at the top with a leader. And a lack of vision is a signal for a gifted mechanic who recognizes it."

Nick began to speak, "Mike, I never told you this, but I didn't feel like I was a hotshot leadership coach at the time. I was afraid too. Being a leadership coach came out of my own need for coaching. I was running a division of Brisbing and working with an outside leadership coach, Jon Brames. I was unceremoniously passed over as the next CEO of Brisbing, and my first instinct was to find another role elsewhere. Jon was the one who encouraged me to work with him for a year before even thinking about doing something like that.

"So I stepped down from Brisbing and gave myself to working with Jon more intensely. Jon thought it would be a helpful experience for me to coach other leaders before reengaging as a potential CEO candidate for another company. So at the time you and I were introduced, I was still feeling the sting of insecurity from being passed over as Brisbing's choice for CEO. But Jon believed in me; Jon would tell me again and again that it was the *way* that I did things that would ultimately lead to my success. Jon pushed for my commitment to being radically and lovingly honest even in the face of a great business leader that I admired. So that's what I did for you. And after a year as a leadership coach, when Brisbing's choice for CEO fell apart, the noise was that Brisbing was thinking about reaching out to me for the role. They did, and the rest is history."

Then Nick turned to Jason, "You see, Jason, that key in your hand. Do you know what it is?"

"It sounds like it's about having clarity about the future," Jason said.

"Vision is the second key, but it only comes with the proper application of the first key, which is service. When you begin thinking about other people and their needs, you begin to have creative vision that is bigger than just your vision for yourself. It becomes what it could be for them, for a better future. Then you act on and share the vision with such clarity that those who follow you can see it for themselves, too. Often when we are without vision for our people, we can begin serving them in small ways. Then bigger vision is revealed to us for them, and we see the steps to get there. Companies and organizations begin dying the day they turn inward towards their own needs and not those of their people or customers. When you saw Dr. Morris today, were you able to see without your contacts?"

"No, not at all," Jason responded.

Nick continued, "Think of vision as being able to see things clearly. If you have selfishness, bitterness, greed, and other vices taking control of your heart, you are not going to be able to see clearly. But when you have a pure heart, the vision will come to you.

"You see, Mike was so consumed with all of his problems that he began leading in fear and selfishness—he was afraid of failing and was leading to not fail more than leading out of care for his people. But once he began serving his team and his customers again, in the little things, slowly the faucet began turning back on . . ."

"The firehose came back," Michael interrupted. "I had to slow down again to clean up the mess I made of my family and leaders. But once that cleared, I began sharing the vision, and the rest is history. I asked Nick to be on the Board, but he said it would change our coaching relationship. He asked me to think about that before I offered it to him. So he has been a great coach—and friend—ever since."

Jason's head was swimming. He remembered how by the time he left NFC, he had lost vision, or at the very best he had murky vision for what his role and the region could be. When there were questions about profitability in the region, he was thinking about survival. He was also thinking about his potential promotion. He was consumed with his region's numbers so that he could gain the attention of the leaders within his company. This was a narrow vision that was too small to include the worlds of his customers and his team.

Then Nick, Michael, and Jason enjoyed a meal—prime, grass-fed steak and fresh lobster—sitting together on the balcony overlooking the park. Nick and Michael shared various leadership stories, and Jason had a front-row seat. Jason knew when to take it all in and listen. This was one of those times. When dinner was complete, Brian came to see them.

"Nick, is it okay if I take Jason? He has a big one tomorrow."

"Of course, Brian, thank you. Jason, please go ahead."

With that, Jason excused himself, thanking Michael and Nick. As he walked towards the elevator, Jason could not believe that he had just sat down with one of the most brilliant yet reclusive leaders in the world.

Brian had said tomorrow was a "big one," and given what had happened today, Jason couldn't even begin to imagine what might be coming next.

8

THE TWO DIRECTIONS

After another night's rest and having successfully completed two days of challenges, Jason was beginning to regain his self-confidence. *I have made it through everything that has been thrown at me so far. It's all going to work out for me. It's all heading in the right direction. I don't know why I was so worried.* He looked at the remaining keys to see if there were any clues as to what was next. He turned the keys over slowly, looking at every edge and detail. He did not want to miss anything this time around. Then he heard a knock at his door.

"Brian, is that you?" Jason asked, anticipating Brian's face at the door.

"It is," Brian said.

Jason let him in and Brian's first words broke up the usual rhythm: "Today will be a little bit different. You are on your own after I drop you off. We are going to Knox University today. You need to be somewhere on that campus by 1:00 p.m., and your job is to figure out where. But you can't be one minute late. If you are late, you will miss and forfeit today's challenge."

"I'm up for it." Jason was beginning to beam with confidence. After all, he had passed the first two challenges. Things were looking up for him.

Brian then drove Jason and dropped him off at the student center at Knox University, which was only about ten minutes from Nick's house. While Jason had not gone to Knox University, he knew it was a prestigious school, and he had driven by the campus before. The campus was distinguished by buildings dedicated by various donors, sprawling lawns, lines of trees, and marble fountains.

Jason was ready for his next mission. Looking at his watch, he saw he had about three hours to figure it all out. *Plenty of time,* he thought.

The first thing that came to Jason's mind was to check for an events calendar in or around the student center. He walked up to the building, made of aluminum and glass, and saw through to the hallway. He walked in through the automatic glass doors. Near the hallway was a flat-screen television with scrolling events for the day and month. He saw two different events scrolling into the screen that could be possible candidates for where he needed to be. The first was "Leadership in the Technology Era" at 1:00 p.m. He saw Barry Blazenby and Paul Porter listed as keynote speakers—names he certainly recognized in the field of leadership. He thought this could easily be where he was supposed to be, but it seemed too easy of a challenge. *There must be some type of twist to this,* he thought. This event was in the Union Building, which per the map was on the far west side of campus. The second event that scrolled up at 1:00 p.m. was an alumni event at the Savant Center, which per the map was on the far east side of campus. *This seems promising. Nick must be a donor of Knox University.*

I have two leads here. Maybe if I go well before each event, I can perform some reconnaissance with those who are setting it up. That's my best shot at figuring out which one Nick would be most likely to attend at 1:00 p.m. There is not much else I can do but go for it.

Jason exited the student center through the automatic glass doors and walked confidently west across campus to the

"Leadership in the Technology Era" event. On the way, he noticed the bright blue skies and fair weather. He wondered why he stayed inside so much working at NFC. When he arrived at the Union Building, he noticed people in blue and white uniforms setting up chairs, tablecloths, and preparing food. He stopped one of them and began asking questions.

"Excuse me, can you tell me more about the event that is here?"

"Sir, what would you like to know?" the man replied, as he placed a chair down and unfolded it.

"I am looking to see if a certain speaker or guest will be here," Jason said.

"I'm afraid I can't help you there. You will need to ask Donna Delber, the event planner, for that type of information," he replied. He began to bring out another chair to unfold.

"Thank you, where would I find her?" Jason asked.

"Donna is busy, very busy. But if you can catch her, this must be your day. Look for a woman wearing a headset dressed in black."

Jason scanned the sea of people in blue and white, looking for the black attire to stand out. In the distance, he spotted a figure moving quickly back and forth inside the Union Building and outside to the patio where the chairs and tables were being set up. As Jason came closer, he saw that it was her. She was a slender woman dressed in a black button-up suit, with rectangular glasses and headphones, looking determinedly at her clipboard.

As she almost ran past him, he asked, "Excuse me, are you Donna?"

"Yes, can I help you with something?" she replied as she continued to walk.

He began to follow her. "Do you know if Nick Savant will be here at 1 p.m.?" he asked.

"He spoke at this event last year as one of the keynotes. He is slated to speak at . . . let's see here . . . 2:30, but I do not have his schedule before that," she replied.

"Thank you, that's very helpful," Jason said.

Without missing a beat, she darted past him.

While this appeared to be a great option, he also needed to check the other event. So he hurried across to the east side of campus to the alumni event. As he approached the Savant Center, he saw an archway of balloons and an army of people in blue and white setting up tables, preparing food, and preparing audiovisual equipment. People's eyes were focused on the tasks before them, and their movements were swift but orderly. As Jason observed the symphony of preparations, he bumped into a server.

"Can I help you?" the server asked.

"Sorry, I'm Jason Irving, and I want to learn a little more about this event," Jason responded. "Do you know if Nick Savant will be coming?"

"Oh Nick? Great man. Great man. I am sure he will be here at some point."

"Do you know when?" Jason asked.

"I couldn't tell you, Mr. Irving, I apologize. But let me see if James our event planner can help." He reached down to a device on his lapel, which connected to a headset. "James, this is Jonathan, over."

Jason faintly heard the sound of a voice coming through the earbud in Jonathan's ear.

"Jonathan, James here."

"When is Mr. Savant coming? Do we have a schedule?" Jonathan asked.

"He is coming but negative on the schedule, Jonathan," James replied.

"Copy that." Then turning to Jason, Jonathan said, "I'm terribly sorry, but the man who would know Mr. Savant's schedule, if anyone would, does not have a timeframe for us. I'm sorry I couldn't be of more assistance. But it is very nice to meet you. Is there anything else I can help you with?"

"No, not at this time. But thanks anyway," Jason responded. *I have two strong possibilities on the opposite sides of campus. Why is it that I have come to a fork in the road that seems impossible to decipher? I have no clue what to do. I guess I'll walk to the middle of the campus and give these options some thought. I have to come up with something. I can't lose this challenge because of something that seems so simple. I don't know what else to do.*

Jason then hurried to the middle of the campus. By the time he arrived there, at the student center where he began, and he checked his watch, it was already 12:35 p.m. He had some time to decide, but not a lot of time. The margin for error was very slim. He had to choose where to be by 1:00 p.m., and one event was on the west, and one was on the east.

As he was thinking, a janitor stopped him.

"Where are you going?" the elderly man asked.

"I don't know, I'm trying to figure it out."

"Well, if you don't know where you are going, you are bound to get there," the man said.

"Thanks for the philosophical analysis," Jason said sarcastically, as he thought, *I have two options, but I'm not sure which one is the best.*

Jason paused for a second. He found himself rethinking what he'd just said, when he'd automatically dismissed the man with an annoyed quip. What he'd learned so far at The Gauntlet resounded in his head. *Servant leadership. Let the vision come to you.*

Slowly, Jason said, "Forgive me, sir, because this may sound crazy, but I'm supposed to be somewhere very soon, and I'm not sure where. One option is on the west side of campus, and the other is on the east side of campus. And if I'm not there by the right time, I will lose out on an opportunity."

The man responded, "Hmm . . . sounds like a tough choice. It's about a fifteen-minute walk either way, so if you are wrong, you can't walk to the other place in time. Well, which one do you think it is?"

"I know Nick Savant is speaking at the leadership event and there is an alumni event at the same time. Since he is an alumnus, he could start his day there."

"Oh!" The man's face lit up. "You know that both of those events are at 1:00 p.m.?"

"Yes . . ." Jason said.

The man continued, "Nick Savant teaches an invite-only class here on leadership. I believe it's at . . . let me think . . . 1:00 p.m. Yes, that's right. But you will need a key to the faculty lounge for access . . . and—"

"Does it look like one of these?" Jason excitedly took his keys out of his pocket and showed him his chain.

"Yes, it does! That third one," the man said.

"Where is the class?"

"It's in 4L, just across there, up from the fountain. You are not too far." The man pointed towards a doorway that was close by.

Jason then walked up to 4L, using his key to get in the door. He breathed a sigh of relief and took a seat. He was sure he was in the right place now. *I can't believe I ran into that man and made it,* he thought.

It was 12:50—and faculty and students began pouring in for what was a standing room only event.

Then Nick Savant entered the room.

He began the class at 1:00 p.m. on the dot and welcomed them.

"Today, we are going to talk about the third key of leadership. It's one of my favorites.

"I see a lot of familiar faces. As an aside, once you finish a class with me, you are a lifetime member. You can come back anytime.

"You see, when I had my first leadership assignment, I thought I knew it all. I thought that I could run circles around other leaders. But then I became terrified by the responsibility, by the thought of taking people in the wrong direction. I was serving others, I had a vision, but to execute that vision, I had to admit that I did not know what I was doing. I often rubbed people the wrong way. I was arrogant and naive, but I didn't know it. Then I lost my confidence when I could not accomplish the vision on my own. When I failed, I became defensive. I was proud. I thought I had arrived. The truth is, you never arrive. You are always arriving.

"But then I learned that the third key of leadership is coachability. I learned that I had to humble myself. Pride preceded every fall in my life. I had to admit that I didn't know where I was going, and I needed help. Maybe you are going through that right now.

"The moment I stopped being willing to learn, I stopped leading effectively.

"I learn new things every day, even today. I work with exceptional leaders, and the truly great ones are always learning. They are humble enough to be coachable—at any level. I remember when Mike Wall became a client—here was this successful visionary who had done more than I ever had, ten years my senior, but he was willing to learn from me. Wherever you are in your journey, keep learning. Keep growing. Keep leading."

Jason began to reflect on his leadership journey. He had made a number of mistakes, and he was failing to learn from them. He had stopped learning and receiving training on leadership. He had a vision and tried to implement the vision by himself, but he failed. And then he became so focused on the day-to-day—on surviving more than anything—that he stopped placing a premium on learning. He had become a reactive, stagnant leader.

After Nick finished speaking, attendees began to go up and ask him different leadership questions.

A man wearing beige slacks and a blue blazer came confidently to the front. "Hi, I'm John Bortles, dean of the business school here at Knox. Mr. Savant, what would you say is the most common mistake you see in leaders, and what is the greatest success you see in leaders?"

"Great question, John. I would say the most common mistake leaders make is not understanding the context in which they are leading. Leading a platoon of men in battle and coaching a team of fifth-graders as a soccer coach will have some different implications, different goals, different skills, different communication styles. You need to adapt as a leader to the context that you are in, so there is no one-size-fits-all approach. It's therefore important to understand that context and what is required of you as a leader in that context. That said, there are keys that I believe anyone can learn to unlock success in leadership in just about any context. As far as greatest success? I would consider that understanding the substance of their legacy. What's within you determines your results; what you leave within others determines your legacy."

A young woman asked another question. "Hi Mr. Savant, my name is Sara Shoreline, and I'm an assistant to the Chair of Philosophy. My question is this: how does leadership apply to me? I don't have any people that report to me. I just support my supervisor."

"Sara, that is an excellent question. I would ask this question in return: do you need a title to be a leader? And the answer I have to say to that is *no*. Leading is helping others become who they have the potential to be. Now, does it help to have a title? Certainly. But I know a janitor who is a retired CEO, and he has an incredible influence on people in his life. He meets with students at 6:00 a.m. before class, and with professors and coaches after classes. He would never tell you that. He decided to spend his life in service to others from a place of anonymity."

It was 2:00 p.m. by the time Nick finished answering several other questions, and he closed by addressing the entire group, saying, "Normally I would stay late to chat with all of you, but I have a couple of events to stop by here on campus. Class dismissed!"

Nick made eye contact with Jason, who he had clearly spotted earlier. "So you made it?"

"A janitor saved me," Jason said. "I think I now know which one."

Nick said, "I'm not surprised. I think by now he knows when he sees an unfamiliar face sweating around 12:30 p.m. on a Tuesday that I have something to do with it. Some leaders will refuse to talk with him, and they end up in the wrong place. And that's okay. They need to learn that anything and anyone can help point them in the right direction—and that they can learn from anything or anyone . . . by the way, I'd like you to be my special guest for a leadership event. I know the other speakers well. So please do come along with me now, but I should make it clear that once we get back to my home tonight, you need to go right to sleep. There is no doubt in my mind that you need all the rest you can get for tomorrow morning. Your next challenge will began at 8 a.m. sharp."

After nodding to signal his understanding of those instructions, Jason accompanied Nick throughout the rest of his day—and while he tried his best to enjoy it, his mind began to lock in on the next challenge.

9

ANSWERING THE BELL

Jason received a knock at 7:00 a.m. the next day. It was Brian, with breakfast in hand.

"Okay, I have oatmeal, bananas, and juice for you. You want to get the best meal possible this morning. I hope you slept well," Brian said.

"I'm good. What are we, hitting the gym today?" Jason asked. He was trying to keep it light.

"Something like that," Brian answered. "We're going to be looking for a way for you to push past your limits today. It's going to be an adventure, I promise you."

They finished up breakfast, and Brian took him on a short trip a few miles away. They pulled up to a shopping center, with a sign about thirty feet off of the ground that read "John's Gym." As they walked inside, Jason noticed people with padded gloves on. Some of them were hitting bags held in suspension from the ceiling. Others were throwing punches at one other.

He noticed one person in particular: an older man with dark skin. He was wearing a shirt that read "Coach." The man was staring intently as another man was punching in a series of combinations.

Jason had always wanted to box, but he had never gotten the chance. He had taken some Brazilian jiu-jitsu lessons when he lived in New York and some hapkido lessons in college. He had also been a high school wrestler. He had one kickboxing training experience with a trainer as well. But of boxing—the sweet science—he never had any experience.

Jason heard the man say, "Okay, beautiful. Give me one, two, slip, three, one."

"Who is that?" Jason asked Brian in an undertone.

Brian said, "That's John Railman, a trainer of champions from Connecticut. His latest champion, the guy he's training now, is Fernando Galbrera. He's a champion in his weight class."

Jason looked at Fernando with admiration. The man had long, lean muscle from the bottom of his calves up to his shoulders. His abdominal muscles were tight with perfect separation. He had arms that looked like chiseled hammers. His face was determined and focused.

Then John looked in their direction and said, "Brian, is it Wednesday already?" He began to place something that looked similar to baseball mitts on his hands, only these mitts were clearly not for catching baseballs. They were for catching punches. As Fernando began to punch John, aiming at those mitts, his punches violently travelled through the air. Each time a punch crashed into John's mitt, there was a snapping thump. John was absorbing the punches, while the sound began to bounce off the walls.

"This is Jason. He's going to be training with us today," Brian said to John.

John nodded his head as he avoided an uppercut from Fernando and moved his mitt directly in place to receive the punch with another crashing thump.

Brian turned to Jason, "I have your gear. You can go ahead and change in the bathroom into these, and I will get your wraps, shoes, and headgear." Brian then handed him bright green trunks and a tank top.

Jason did not want to show any fear, but this was all very new to him. He was out of his element and saw people that were clearly trained and much more experienced than him at this sport. While he was a competitor in many aspects of his life, he dealt with fear throughout most of it. One of his greatest fears was failure, as well as being criticized. He could still remember the sting of losing in sports or getting less than As in classes. After he changed into his trunks and tank top, he went and found Brian.

Brian took out a roll of thin, bright red cloth strips. He wound them around Jason's wrists, and then around his thumbs, wrapping them across the palms of his hands. He then wrapped them in between Jason's fingers and then back around his palms and wrists before wrapping them between the next set of fingers. Brian chatted with Jason as he worked. "So I don't know much about you and your wife. Tell me about her."

Jason began to relax a bit as he answered the question. "Shaunny? She is amazing and supportive. She loves people. She invests all of her time in helping them . . ." Jason's mind was wandering as he tried to answer Brian. *Did I eat enough breakfast? How's my water intake? What about my old shoulder injury?*

"Okay, how do those feel?" Brian asked after both hands were wrapped.

"These feel good, I think. Let's go for it!" Jason answered. *What did I get myself into? Shaunny is going to kill me if I break my nose. But I am going to learn how to box!*

"Great, I am going to get wrapped up and will join you soon. Just relax. Here's water for you," Brian said.

Nearby, John was apparently finishing up with Fernando. "Great work, Fernando. Hit the speed bag and stretch, and you are done for the morning," John said.

"Thanks, Coach," said Fernando.

John then stepped out of the ring, removed his mitts, and came over to Jason.

"Jason, I'm Coach John."

"Good to meet you," Jason responded. *Oh no, what am I doing here? What is about to happen?*

"Any experience in the ring?" John asked.

"No, not really. Dabbled in mixed martial arts, but no boxing," Jason responded. *That's right, I have mixed martial arts experience. I am letting you know that . . . but I hope you don't figure out it was only a year's worth!*

"I train champions and kids, and everything in between," said John. Then, with a grin that was not unkind, he added, "I can see you are the in-between. Let's get started with stretching. It's important to stay loose, stretched, and warm. Let's start with your neck." John rolled his neck clockwise with his chin down to his chest. "Start clockwise," he instructed. Then after three revolutions, John reversed the direction. "Now the other side."

John continued with three revolutions, and Jason watched and followed. *This isn't so bad,* he thought.

"Now I want you to touch your chin to your chest. And then move it back and look up at the ceiling."

Jason kept following along.

"Now try to touch your ear to your shoulder; start with your right and then go to the left."

Jason felt the muscles in his neck beginning to relax.

John continued to take Jason through a series of stretches, starting with his neck, down to his hips and hamstrings. John clearly believed in correct preparation to avoid injury.

"Okay, let's start with the jump rope." John took the rope and began loosely jumping back and forth from one foot to the other, smoothly allowing the rope to come under his feet just as his feet left the ground. The rope was swinging around in a consistent beat. John's face was without stress or strain. His muscles were relaxed and focused. "Just relax and wait for the bell. When it rings, you will have three minutes, and at the second bell there will be thirty seconds left. The key is to develop a rhythm."

When the first bell came, Jason took the rope and began jumping up and down with his feet crashing against the mat. The rope would smack against his ankles in the front or he would step on it.

"Okay, Jason, not so fast. Pace yourself. You have a couple of rounds of this," John interrupted.

After a mere minute, Jason was dripping with sweat down his chest and forehead. Not only was he experiencing accumulated mental exhaustion from the challenges this week, but now he was training at a high intensity that he had not reached in a long time. His training regimen had fallen off a bit since he got married. Then it was two minutes in, and he was feeling the burn in his legs. By the time there were thirty seconds left, he was gasping for air.

When the final bell hit, Jason felt as if he were ready to pass out.

"Okay, good, Jason. Good. You have a minute till the next bell. Get hydrated," John said.

Jason continued to sweat like he was leaking. The sweat was travelling down his tank top and to his trunks. After two more rounds of jump rope, Jason's clothes were soaked, his lungs were burning as if they were on fire, and his legs were like loose noodles, ready to buckle under him. *They cannot see me like this. Stay up, Jason. Stay up,* he thought.

Jason instinctively reached for some water and began to drink. He felt his hand on the cold bottle, and as he lifted it to his lips, the water came down his throat smoothly and soothed the pain he was in for a few moments.

"Jason, now that you're done warming up, let's start with the basic stance. You are going to stand with your feet shoulder width apart," John said, taking the stance himself and motioning for Jason to follow.

"Now place your left foot a small step in front. Turn your body back clockwise about thirty degrees. Okay, now place your left hand and right hand at your cheeks. It's important to keep yourself protected at all times."

Jason was attempting to move with John's instructions. He found himself tripping with his feet and awkwardly placing his hands by his chin. John grabbed Jason's elbows and moved him and his hips into the proper place.

"That's better," John said. "It's all about balance. Now your hands at your cheeks—at your cheeks!"

Jason moved his hands up.

"Okay, now, you are going to stand slightly up on your toes with your legs bent. Chin down."

Jason followed instructions, though his calves began shaking.

"Beautiful!" John said. "Let's get started. Boxing is technique. Technique is boxing. The power—it's from your hips, not your arms. Stay light on your feet.

"Let's start with the jab. You twist your hip first. Try that motion."

Jason moved his hips like he was dancing, but his limbs and his trunk were not moving in unison.

"Not that much," John said. "Now after you move your hips slightly clockwise, you send out your arm with your fist tight. Now aim at my face."

John moved his arm and fist out.

"Wait, Jason. Hips first. Remember?"

"Right, right," Jason said.

Jason moved his hips, and then as he moved his arm and fist out, it was going straight towards John. John moved slightly out of the way.

"Very good, Jason," he encouraged.

John began taking Jason through the different punches—jab, cross, and the hook. He took him through some basic defense as well: the slip, bob, and weave.

"Jason, it's time for some bag work. Get your gloves on. Now I will call out combinations. One means jab, two means cross, three means hook. Got it?"

Jason was tired but he was enjoying this learning. *Anything but the jump rope*, he thought. "Sure, let's go."

"One. Two. One . . . one, two . . . one, two . . . one, two, three. Stay in your stance now."

John kept calling out numbers, and Jason kept swinging and panting. Then John said, "You have potential, Jason. But you're overthinking! You have to just let it fly. And when you finish a combination, return to your stance."

After three rounds, Jason was tired but energized.

"Alright, Jason, it's time for sixes. You are going to punch the bag six times. One-two, one-two, one-two. Then hit the bag with a hook. You try."

Jason hit the bag with his left and then his right hand three times. Then he curved his left hand around for the hook.

"That's one rep . . . okay, let me show you . . . Fernando! Come over here and show Jason how it's done."

When the bell rang, Fernando began throwing rapid punches back-to-back, though he did not move from the area of his stance.

"Okay . . . 139, 140 . . . great work, Fernando," John said. Then he turned to Jason. "It's as easy as that. Let's see what you got!"

At the bell, Jason came to the bag and began hitting it, first with his left, and then with his right, and then with a left hook. After thirty reps, his arms, shoulders, legs, and body were burning, full of lactic acid. He could barely move.

They were cheering him on though. Everyone clearly knew it was hard enough, being as it was his first time. "Keep going, Jason, Keep going!" John and Brian yelled. Finally, the bell rang.

"Thirty-eight reps," John said. "Not bad, Jason, get some water."

Not an inch of what Jason was wearing was dry. After he drank the cool water, he hit the ground.

"Get up, Jason, get up! We have two more rounds," John said.

Two more *rounds. This is crazy. Who would do this? Who would willingly subject himself to this?* Jason wondered. Then he answered himself, *I guess I am!* He was desperate for change and would try anything; that was why he was here.

Jason felt he was being pushed to his maximum. During the second round, he could barely break thirty reps. By the third round, he pushed just to get to thirty. Physically, he was done. He could not keep going. He wanted to quit. And then he felt something unpleasant in his stomach. It was his breakfast fighting with itself. He headed over to the trash can to prepare for what seemed inevitable. The trash can looked very appealing at this point since he could not hold his breakfast down any longer. After wrapping his arms around the trash can, he vomited his breakfast.

It was a relief. After wiping his mouth with his shirt, he walked back over to the heavy bag, hoping John would have mercy on him and end the session.

"Alright, Jason. You're good," John said.

As soon as he said it, Jason knew John was intending for him to continue.

"I'm done. I can't go anymore," Jason said. He couldn't believe that his hopes for mercy had gone unanswered.

"Get some water. You have three minutes of rest. Then you need to spar," John said. He grinned. "There's no way I'm depriving you of the entire experience, son!"

Where is the mercy? Jason wondered. *I am going to die here! This is it. I am going to die in a boxing gym, and I haven't even been hit by a punch!* His mind began racing. At this point, he was ready to die.

At least he had a good life insurance policy—he knew Shaunny would be taken care of.

Jason nodded towards John, as if saying, *You are legally responsible for anything that happens to me next. You are going to have to take care of my wife when I'm gone.*

"Okay, let's get his head gear on," Brian said, coming to attend to him. Then the door to the gym opened, and Nick Savant walked in. Nick looked at Jason.

Jason looked back, drenched in sweat, his legs shaking under him.

"Perfect!" Nick said. "It looks like you're doing great. This is where the rubber meets the road, my friend. This is where you get to see who you are when all of the layers are peeled back, and it's just you, on your last leg, and still facing a fight. Now we get to see who you are at your core." Nick nodded to John and added, "Thanks for taking him on."

John nodded back and then said, "Jason, get in the ring. You are going to spar. I promise we're not going to put you in the hospital! But we are not going to go easy either. We are going to push you to the end of your limits . . . and then past that."

"I don't know if I can even stand up," Jason responded. He was still hoping for some mercy.

"Get in the ring, Jason. Get in," John said, holding the ropes open for him.

Jason got in the ring, gingerly. His feet were burning. He was disoriented.

"Brian, you are up first," John said. Brian darted in through the ropes and began jumping back and forth from one foot to the other, twisting his hips and placing his hands in front of him with a series of punches. In all of Jason's jumble of emotions—fear, anger, and despair—he managed to have hope that he had treated Brian well the last couple of days. *I hope I was not a jerk these last few days,* Jason thought. *Otherwise he's going to demolish me.*

"Wait for the bell," John said. *Bing.* The round started.

"Touch gloves," John instructed. Brian reached out with his glove and Jason begrudgingly tapped it with his glove.

Brian then jabbed Jason in the face.

John was shouting instructions. "Gloves to your cheeks, Jason. Gloves to your cheeks!"

Jason was woozy, and fell over.

"Don't go out like that, Jason! Get up!" shouted Nick. "Everybody falls, but not everybody gets back up!"

Jason pulled himself up by the ropes. The hit and force were not what had brought him down. It was the weariness in his legs, the sogginess of his mind. Jason was having trouble thinking straight.

Brian continued to charge Jason. Jason tried protecting his head this time, and Brian then came in with two shots to Jason's ribs. Down again went Jason. The shots were not, Jason was sure, as hard as Brian *could* punch, but they were so direct that the force didn't matter.

Jason again attempted to summon everything he had to get up, but his energy was spent. After a few more seconds, the bell rang.

"Okay, Jason, round one is over. Next up is Nick," John said.

John looked into Jason's eyes, but Jason couldn't hold his gaze. He'd lost heart. He felt defeated.

Jason was then surprised to see Nick coming into the ring. Jason felt like he was heading to a funeral.

His own.

Bing. The bell went off.

I just need to make it out alive, Jason thought.

Nick came in close, and Jason tried to hug him so that he would not have to box. Nick swiftly ducked under his arms and gave Jason a crisp shot to his solar plexus. His glove smacked with a thump against it. Jason went down again. This time he just lay on the floor.

"Get up, Jason. Get up!" shouted John.

But Jason was completely exhausted. He lay on the floor for about seven seconds. Then he turned on his stomach and pressed his shaking arms against the floor to prop himself up. He managed to stumble onto his feet.

Jason was confused, bewildered even. He was not sure where he was.

They began fighting again. Jason, in a last-ditch attempt at actually connecting, tried to throw a jab-cross combination, but he was off balance and fell in the ring. He then pressed himself back onto his feet. Nick gave him a jab to the head. Down Jason went again . . . then the bell rang.

"Jason, come here, let's get you some water," John said from the corner.

Jason drank the cool water, still thinking he was about to pass out. Things were so fuzzy and hazy; he was not thinking clearly. There was no mercy in this ring.

Bing. The bell rang.

"Okay, round three," John said.

Then into the ring came Fernando.

"You are kidding me," Jason said. "This is crazy."

Fernando began dancing around the ring, looking ready to pounce. Jason was terrified. He quit in his heart.

Then, at that moment, Nick stopped the training. "Okay, that's enough, Jason. You are done. Great work today. Get some water. Take a few minutes."

Jason was exhausted, humiliated, and wiped out.

John took him through some final stretches and checked his eyes to make sure he was okay. There was no damage, just weariness and exhaustion. Jason had never been worked out that hard in his life.

Then John spoke. "Jason, do you know what just happened?"

"Yeah. I got my rear end kicked."

"Let me tell you something about boxing. It's about skill and endurance. I train my guys to feel out their opponents for the first few rounds and let the opponents wear themselves out. Once they are completely exhausted, then they go for the kill. There was no way you were going to survive today. No one does. In boxing, when you get hit or when you fall, you rise up again. It takes courage, and it takes grit to be a boxer.

"But it also takes training. You can't just walk into the ring without respecting the ring. It takes years to hone this craft, to build the endurance, to have the right mental attitude."

Jason, as the fog cleared, realized how much he was afraid of failure. It drove him more than he wanted to admit or realize. But in this moment, he had just failed at something and realized that this was the same pattern he'd seen throughout his days of leadership in his career.

Nick added, "Do you know how often leaders get into the ring without having a full appreciation for the training, experience, and endurance it takes? Boxing is a lot like leadership in that you are going to get hit. First, you need the courage to enter that ring, but you also need to be as prepared as possible because you do not rise to your level of leadership; you fall to your level of training. Those critical moments in leadership are going to come down to your training and preparation. There was no way you were *not* going to fail today. Today you needed to fail because in leadership you will face failure. But you must have the courage to continue, to carry on with your purpose."

John said, "It's not that my best fighters don't fail. They do. It's that they are as prepared as possible, humble enough to respect the ring and their opponent, and because of this, they put the training in necessary to endure the hits and the blows that are going to come. They train hard so that in the time of crisis they fall back on their training instincts. When we prepare for a fight, we train with every scenario possible. And yet . . . they don't always win. They might lose a fight here or there. They still have the courage to get back into the ring. That's a fighter. A fighter is not someone who always wins but someone who loses and has the courage to fight again."

As Jason thought about it, he saw he had lost the courage to get back in the ring. What happened today felt like some of his weeks at NFC. He was weary, in a daze, and was getting knocked down because he was not trained and prepared for it. He had lost his courage, his mojo.

"And by the way," Nick said, "No one ever fights Fernando. You were not going to fight Fernando today. That would have been malpractice on our part. But, if you put the training and time in, and dedicated yourself to the craft, one day you *could* spar with him."

"Jason, you can train here anytime," John said. "When I had my first gym, I was having trouble with my landlord. I was getting ready to throw in the towel. When word got around to Nick that chains were about to go onto the front doors, Nick spoke with my landlord and purchased the building. He made him an offer he wouldn't refuse. Nick gave me the first year of rent free, and that's how I got back on my feet. And now, business has never been better. Anyone good with Nick is good with me. Nick has a key to this place, and so should you."

Nick said, "Jason, the fourth key of leadership, if you haven't figured it out yet, is courage. Failure is going to happen over and over again, but it's your preparation and your willingness to face your fears that are the key to accessing the courage within you to enter the ring again. Go ahead and take out your keys."

Jason pulled them off the bench and showed them to Nick and John.

"It's that one," John said, pointing at the silver key. Jason nodded, overwhelmed by the entire experience. "Nick, I don't know what to say. I have been in so much fear these past few weeks. To hear your words gives me the courage to enter the ring again. Recently, I doubted whether I even wanted to be a leader. I was running on a false confidence, and now I have come crashing back to earth. I realize I have a lot of work to do."

Nick put his hand on Jason's shoulder, "That's courage. Facing yourself and not blaming others for any failures in your leadership . . . now let's get you a meal and some clean clothes."

With that, they left John's Gym and headed back to Nick's estate. Jason was thankful he would not have to go back to the gym for the rest of the day. He just wanted to pass out on the couch. And he did, after lunch and a shower.

Jason woke up from his nap to a splitting headache and a whole-body ache. *That must be normal,* he thought. And while his old shoulder injury ached, it didn't feel like he'd done himself any new harm there. He then heard a knock at the door. Jason went to answer the door and open it for Brian when—

Nick came in.

"I thought you were Brian," Jason said, startled by Nick's presence. He was especially intimidated after the boxing experience.

"No, I came to tell you I'm proud of how far you have come over these past few days. I am proud of the way you have faced these challenges and learned these keys to leadership. But now there is one more key for you to learn. And you will have forty-eight hours on the property to figure out what it is. At the end of forty-eight hours, I want to know what the last key is. See you in a few days."

With that, Nick shut the door, and Jason was all alone. He was too tired to reflect on what might be coming next—on how he was going to solve the puzzle Nick had just left for him. He lay down on his bed. His eyes began to close, and then he fell asleep.

10

The End of the Rope

Jason woke up the next morning, his body aching. His legs, his abdominals, and his shoulders were burning. He rolled out of bed and gingerly began to stand up. The sunlight sneaking through the window hit his eyes, blinding him. He placed the inside of his hand on top of his brow to soften the beam of light coming in. As he regained his sight, he could hear high-pitched chirping coming from outside. He walked over to the blinds and placed his hand in between two levels of blinds, spreading them open. He noticed three little birds bobbing their heads, fluttering, and circling one another. The chirps were happy sounds, playful sounds. As much as his body hurt him, he began to appreciate the little play nature was putting on for him.

This is an adventure, he thought. *Why not explore some more?* He let go of the blinds and walked out of his room, stumbling upstairs around the winding staircase and into the second bedroom to get a better look from a higher vantage point. As he walked towards the window, he saw that within the bedroom, on the left, there was another door, one he had overlooked.

There was a carved, wooden sign hanging over that door. The sign read, "The Sanctuary."

Jason put aside his fascination with nature for a moment and placed his hand on the doorknob. He could feel the coolness of the brass against his sore hand. It was therapeutic. He slowly twisted the doorknob, pulling open the door. He looked into the room, which was dimly lit, and inhaled the fresh smell of the wooden bench and panels. He saw pictures on the wall of grand mountainous landscapes, beaches, and gardens; a small circular table had fresh, white candles upon it; and another table was set with what looked like paint brushes and a blank canvas.

There was also a journal and pen sitting there, as if inviting him. *I guess I could pause and reflect here, but I'm on a mission,* Jason thought. He took his keys out of his pocket and looked at them. What he'd learned so far at The Gauntlet replayed in his head. *Servant leadership. Let the vision come to you. Be coachable. Find courage to face failure.* One of them had a meaning yet to be revealed to him. He inspected the last key, looking for clues. It seemed a plain gold key with no differentiating marks.

Why am I here? What am I supposed to do next? He explored more, looking for additional places and clues for his key. He walked through both floors, inspecting, thinking, and searching. *Nothing. I can't find any clues in front me. What does this have to do with leadership anyway?*

He then walked back downstairs, opening the door to head outside. He began walking briskly up to every statue in the garden, around every plant, walking in circles looking for clues to the mystery of the next key. Between his body aching and the mental exhaustion, he was ready to complete this training and be done. *I'm done with this. I'm ready to quit. Forget it. It's not worth it.*

Summoning his last ounce of willpower, he spent a few more hours inspecting outside the property. To his disappointment, he did not find any additional clues.

By the time the sun went down, Jason was completely weary. *Let me get a good night's rest. That will solve it. There's nothing more that I can do tonight, or I will completely wear myself out,* he thought.

Sometimes solutions to problems would come to Jason when he would step away from trying to solve the problem himself.

After eating potatoes, broccoli, and half a piece of chicken breast, he was full. Even though that was a small meal for him, he did not want to eat any more; his stomach was tying itself in knots. The sun having gone down, he looked at his bed and decided to get an early night's rest. He changed into sweats and a t-shirt. He then closed his eyes, but rest escaped him. He tossed and turned most of the night, sleeping only a few hours. He was sweating, unable to sleep. His mind was racing. *I hate it when this happens. I can't turn my mind off.* It reminded him of when he was a young man in college, when he had trouble sleeping due to his high anxiety. He had even taken medication for a time to address the issue. This was all a painful reminder of those times. He was feeling like a failure . . . again. This was a feeling he tried to run from most of his life, but it always seemed to catch up with him. *Here I go again. I thought I was the man, but clearly I'm not. It's failure all over again. I'm a failure,* he thought.

He began to hear the faint sounds of chirping. The black of night began lightening. The last day was coming upon him. He got out of bed, and with a forced burst of tired energy, he immediately began retracing his steps from the prior day, searching for clues to the last key. He went through all the drawers and cabinets. He went outside, searching more. There were no clues. It seemed hopeless. *Failure again. See, it always catches up with me. This is what I always do,* he thought.

He paused and let that repeated thought sink in. Then, another thought suddenly came into his mind. He was . . . away.

From life. From busyness. From himself. From his responsibilities.

He was alone.

He noticed a rusted and empty fountain just outside the door. It was a place where life once flowed.

Jason began to experience an emptiness. It felt like a lonely, dark cavern. He was afraid of what he would find when he entered this place of his soul. It seemed like the shadow of his soul, shielded from the light of life. *This darkness is the source of the busyness in my life. This is the place that drives me. I am afraid of experiencing this utter emptiness of stopping, and that is why my life is in perpetual motion,* he thought.

Jason began to experience a crushing weight. He began feeling the responsibility he owed to his wife, to the people he led—of the weight of the purpose of his life unfulfilled. He began thinking about his past failures in school, in business, in relationships, with friends, with himself. *I did not realize how much of the past I am carrying with me,* he thought. *These suitcases keep unpacking themselves. It feels like a whirlwind of worry, regret, and fear. Why am I feeling this? I hate this . . .*

There was a swirling wind of anxious thoughts like a hurricane—unannounced, unwelcome, and uninvited.

He stumbled back inside. He lay down for a few minutes. *Okay, calm down, calm down,* he thought. *But what can I do? There must be something I can do. But if I can't figure out what to do, how am I going to find this key? This is going to be another failure.* He felt a continual pain and uneasiness in his heart and body. He was desperate for a sense of peace that was eluding him.

Then something within him led him to go back upstairs. He walked gingerly up the stairs and came to the room. He noticed the sign "The Sanctuary" again. He walked up to the door, opening it. As he went in, he looked again at the landscapes, the tables, the candles, and the painting supplies. He smelled the fresh scent of wood, and the slightest scent of the vanilla candles, though they were unlit. It was quiet. He could think. And then his eyes were drawn to several framed signs within, signs he had not noticed before. They read:

> You're blessed when you're at the end of your rope.
> With less of you there is more of God and his rule.
>
> You're blessed when you're content with just who you are—no more, no less.
> That's the moment you find yourselves proud owners of everything that can't be bought.

You're blessed when you get your inside world—your mind and heart—put right.

Then you can see God in the outside world.[1]

When Jason saw these words, he felt a lightness inside him, a sense of ease. *There is nothing for me to do,* Jason thought. *Only rest in God.*

"God" was not a word that Jason had thought about, much less said in years. Sure, he had heard about God as a child, from his father who spoke of the God of Abraham, Isaac, and Jacob. His mother would talk about Jesus Christ, the Son of God. He had been to synagogue. He had been to church. He had attempted meditation. He had read books by the Dalai Lama. But Jason was burnt out on all religion.

I'm at the end of my rope. I have been so discontent with myself and with life. My inside world is not right. I'm so tired, he thought.

His eyes then saw a small framed sign in the corner. It read:

But they who wait for the Lord shall renew their strength.[2]

His anxiety was beginning to lift. *But,* he thought, *I cannot focus on renewal. I must focus on waiting, trusting, hoping, expecting from God.* His eyes then saw a small sign on the opposite side of the wall:

On the day I called, you answered me; my strength of soul you increased.[3]

He had never really prayed in his life. But words began to come out of his mouth that he could hardly believe.

"God, if you are there, I need help. I have been running life on my own power. I'm at the end of my rope. I'm not content with who I am or with my life. My inside world—my heart and mind—are not right. I am weak, and I am calling upon you to strengthen me. I do not want to do this in my own power anymore. Help me."

Then there was silence. The moments seemed like hours. He felt the tension lifting from his body and muscles.

He gazed upon two pieces of wood in The Sanctuary. One was vertical and the other was placed horizontally across it, making the shape of a cross. There was a plaque beneath these pieces of wood that said:

> I have been crucified with Christ. It is no longer I who live, but Christ who lives in me. And the life I now live in the flesh I live by faith in the Son of God, who loved me and gave himself for me.[4]

Jason began thinking more, and what he thought seemed to come from a source outside of him.

Jesus Christ is with me. This deep belief is soaking into my soul right now—to the marrow and bone. That same Jesus who came to live as a human, lived a life without sin, was crucified, buried, and then raised to life—and I with him. That Jesus is with me. I sense an angel with me. I am protected.

Wait, but is all of this real? he wondered. He stepped outside into nature to be sure. He was feeling a new energy coursing through his body. As he gazed upon the beauty of creation—the trees, the birds, the flowers, the mountain ranges ahead—he felt an energy in his soul. He thought about driving home at that moment, but he wanted to reflect more about this trip and what was happening to him.

He had begun untying his soul from the incessant demands of the world.

My mind has been saturated with negativity. I have been hurried as a leader beyond the speed limit of my soul. I have been addicted to the adrenaline-fueled pace of life as a leader.

It was hard to believe, but it was already six in the evening. He was feeling refreshed and relaxed. He was looking forward to enjoying life again. He had been tied to his phone, to e-mail, to the world. And now he was free. In all this new thought, he was not sure what the last key was about, but neither did he seem to care. He walked back inside to The Sanctuary. There was something pulling him to journal.

He picked up a fountain pen, sat down, and began to write.

What is happening to me? What is this sudden change? I feel lighter. I feel as if a heaviness has been lifted. This is not some magical incantation. But I feel lighter. It's all so clear. I was leading in my own strength and power. I became the type of self-reliant leader that I despised, heading towards self-destruction, unaware of the consequences. I have been saved from the ill fate of that leadership life!

He looked up from the journal and peered out the window at the mountains and tree line before him.

All seems to be right in this world. I cannot put my finger on it, but something has changed in my heart. I have a new faith. I have a new hope. I can rest.

With that, he got out of The Sanctuary, and he took his journal with him to bed. As he lay down on his back, his eyes began to feel the weight of the lack of sleep, of his weariness. His eyes shut, and he fell asleep.

The next morning, Jason woke up refreshed. He was calm. He was reflecting upon his experience. And he heard a knock. He approached the door and opened it. Nick was at the door announcing, "Jason, it's time to let me know the last key."

Jason responded with glowing excitement, "I don't know what happened to me over our time together. When I first got here, I was so focused on winning and figuring out the challenges of the keys. But after the last forty-eight hours, I realize there is more work on the inside of me going on right now. I spent a lot of time reflecting about my leadership and my life. I even said a short prayer yesterday. I am feeling refreshed and energized.

"And Nick, I am sorry," he continued. He took the keychain out of his hand and pointed to the fifth key. "I do not know what this key is for. On the first day, I looked everywhere on the property for the answer. But then I spent the second day reflecting on my leadership and life. I am feeling energized and strengthened, but I am not sure if I have been in a healthy place to be a leader. So much of my leadership was about me, relying on my strength, for my notoriety, for my success. And I think it burned me out. But I found something more valuable."

"And what's that?" Nick asked.

"I think God brought me here to get me to the end of my rope and to get my heart put right," Jason answered. It was the first time he acknowledged that he had a heart issue and verbalized his own self-reliance. And it was freeing. His fear of criticism and failure melted away as he spoke the words.

Nick said, "I think you're right, Jason. I see your eyes glowing with a divine spark. I see God's image renewed within you. That image was there before, but it was marred. I think you are beginning to see the invaluable treasure that God has placed within you.

"And that, Jason, is where we come to the final key. The last key is the key of transformation. Leaders need to be challenged so that they can be transformed. And that key comes from and belongs to God. It's nothing I can do or give you. There is nothing more powerful than a transformed leader who serves, has vision, is willing to learn, and has the courage to face failure. But it's the key of transformation that is the most important.

"Jason, whether you believe in God or not, every leader has been made in his image. That image may be corrupted, broken, or marred, but that image is still there. Now the gifts God has given us? We may choose not to use them for his purposes. I believe that true leadership is theocratic leadership, meaning that leadership is given by God for the sake of others. Leadership is from God and for the purpose of loving him and loving others. If any areas of our life are out of alignment with those purposes, there will be a leadership pathology. Many leaders are self-aggrandizing, using leadership for their own gain, power, prestige, and wealth. That's why leaders need to be transformed. They often need to be challenged into transformation. And God is the greatest coach and challenger of all. He will coach you hard. But then he will love you harder afterwards. Most of a leader's problems, failures, and challenges are disguised opportunities for transformation, but a leader needs to give himself to the process. Very few ever do, and it usually takes something large and something painful happening in their lives—like it did with you—to bring leaders to the end of their ropes."

Jason stood there, motionless, taking it all in. He saw in Nick something he was longing for. He saw strength, but he also saw love. He felt Nick's love in that moment piercing through his soul. It was an intense love that seemed to burn up Jason's insecurities.

Jason responded, "Nick, I know you are right. I know you speak the truth. I have been resisting it for so long. I was afraid to fail. I was afraid to change. But now, I know that if I weren't at the end of my rope, I would not have let God in."

"I'm glad you're feeling encouraged, Jason," said Nick, his expression turning serious, "but I also need to warn you. You're in a critical position right now, and I've seen many leaders before you in this same position. Some of them impulsively threw themselves into the next challenge to avoid the painful self-awareness of this experience.

"Because of their examples, I can tell you what *not* to do next. Don't jump into your next leadership role or project right away. Take some time to reflect on this past week and over your career in these areas: service, vision, coachability, courage, and transformation. Have you become self-centered in your leadership? That is an indication of a need to serve. Are you lacking vision? That may be a good indication that you have lost sight of what's most important. You should take some time to rest and reflect on what matters and who you are serving. Have you stopped growing as a leader? It's time to talk with mentors, get a coach, read books, take classes. Start learning and sharpening your skills. Have you become reticent or fearful in your leadership? It's time to take risks where failure could be the result. Practice making decisions and facing failure on a regular basis. Has it been a long time since you have had transformation? Get alone and reflect with God. Create some intentional space to reflect, to let your heart catch up to what you have been experiencing. This is just the beginning for you of this transformed life as a leader. Take advantage of this time off to recalibrate and reconnect with the God who made you and called you into leadership."

As he listened to Nick, Jason knew he would never have faced these questions before this week. But with his crash course in the keys of leadership, Jason had a new level of confidence to do this deeper work. "Thank you, Nick. Thank you for what you have done for me. My heart is full of gratitude."

Nick said, "Jason, you have done some great work this week—hard work, challenging work. Yet this is just the beginning of the journey. You are welcome to stay as long as you need to here, and you are welcome to come back whenever you need a refresher. And I want you to send leaders over. Send someone who needs to be challenged and believed in."

Jason saw that Nick lived up to his reputation. He was an intense leader! But the intensity was not without love. Nick walked over, and for the first time wrapped his arms around Jason and pulled him in for a close hug. He then looked Jason in the eyes and said, "Jason, remember this: God will coach you hard, but then afterwards, he will love you harder! Keep the keys of leadership with you to remind you that you have within you what you need to face the challenges ahead."

Tears began welling up in Jason's eyes. It was rare for him to experience challenge and love at the same time. He did not know how much he needed this experience. He could not remember the last time he was believed in. He loved what he was experiencing, though he did not fully understand it.

"Jason, I am going to leave you to yourself for the rest of the day. That will give you time to reflect on this experience," Nick said.

Nick then left and shut the door behind him. Jason sat down on a chair for a moment.

Looking back, Jason saw how his drive for recognition and promotion had pulled him away from service. He had become self-centered. The fear of losing recognition and the promotion had clouded his vision, which was more about himself than other people. He had then become obsessed with advancing and had stopped resting and caring for himself and his wife the way he wanted. He remembered cancelling a vacation with his wife in the last year so that he could work more. He had thought he knew it all. He'd stopped learning and growing. He had become timid in his leadership, more motivated by avoiding failure and criticism than fueled by his purpose. He had resisted the call from God to be transformed. He had been afraid of being exposed if he admitted he needed to change.

For this reflection, though, Jason was grateful. He was looking forward to leading again with these new keys of leadership. He sensed that his training was complete and it was time for him to go home. Shaunny probably was wondering how he was doing anyway. He packed up and took his keys with him, reflecting on the Leadership Gauntlet with appreciation.

And then he remembered the armoire, and all the thank-you cards. Now it was his turn to thank Nick.

He walked upstairs and into the living room. He opened up the armoire. He looked more closely at the cards of those who had been here before—current CEOs, leaders, senators, pastors, coaches of professional sports teams. His eyes looked and saw a thank-you card from Bill Benton, his former supervisor and CEO at NFC. It read:

> Dear Nick,
>
> I came here burned out, depressed, afraid, and demoralized. I never realized how hard it was for me to do the right thing, to have courage to tell people the truth, to have courage to ask for what I need. I will never forget what you did for me this week. A few years ago, I had a leader under my care, and I never told him the truth of what I saw in him. He was extremely talented and gifted, but there were areas of his character that gave me concern. When he was selected to become CEO of another organization, the sleeping dragons I saw in him but was too afraid to confront him about came alive. After several years, he was not able to handle the pressure. He had a heart attack, an affair with his secretary, and was divorced within three years of obtaining the role. He spent the end of his days addicted to drugs, but he still managed to attend conference calls and somehow function. After missing several meetings, the Board became concerned and reached out to his ex-wife. She came back to their house, only to find him dead from an overdose

in his mansion. I never got over that one. It wasn't until after my week here with you that I began to address how the lack of transformation in my life was affecting my leadership. This has been a transformational week for me and a watershed moment in my career. I vow that the next time I see a promising, young leader, I will have the courage to present him with the truth.

Sincerely,
Bill

Jason was shocked to read this, but it suddenly made sense. Bill wasn't a born fearless leader like everyone thought. And it was not that he didn't believe in Jason. He saw potential in Jason, but he did not want Jason to be seduced by the allure of leadership. Jason saw now that Bill must have loved and cared for him enough that he did not want him promoted to a level that his heart and character could not sustain. Bill believed in him all along—and loved him and Shaunny enough to do this for him. All this time Jason had been angry with Bill and with God, and now he saw that it was God who saved him from himself, using Bill as a means to do it. Jason had clarity.

With a sense of perspective and gratitude, Jason picked up a pen and wrote his own thank-you card.

Dear Nick,

Thank you for taking the time to challenge and believe in me when I had lost belief in myself. You will never know how much I appreciate what this week has meant for me. I came here a self-serving, myopic, prideful, fearful leader, unwilling and afraid to change. I leave here a transformed one, and I know that there is more progressive change ahead. But with God, all things are possible.

Sincerely,
Jason

With that, Jason closed the armoire. He began thinking about the legacy he would leave. He looked at the keys in his hand and began having vision for being a servant, visionary, teachable, courageous, and transformed leader. He thought about his future, the type of leader he would become, and who he might eventually send here to undertake a similar journey. He walked downstairs with a confident sense of purpose, taking hold of his suitcase. He walked out slowly, soaking in the moment and then closing the door behind him. But he was not the same person, not the same leader.

The transformation had begun.

11

THE CALL

Jason drove home with a sense of passion and purpose. Normally, he would turn his phone on, listen to the news, and communicate with his wife, family, and friends, but he wanted some silence to take this all in.

Finally, about halfway through the drive, he could not help himself. He dialed Shaunny.

When she picked up the phone, he greeted her. "Shaunny!"

"Jason, babe, I have been wondering when you would call. Are you okay?" Shaunny replied.

"I'm okay. In fact, I'm more than okay."

"Jason, you would not believe it, but our landline has been ringing like crazy."

"Really?"

"Paul Norman. Michael Wall. Jon Brames. They are all coming out of the woodwork. And they want you. You have to hear some of the messages. There are offers. You have to hear this, Jason!"

"What! You are kidding me."

"No, I'm serious, Jason. They want you. Let me play one."

Jason then heard the robotic voice of the answering machine.

"You have eleven messages. First message."

He then heard a man's voice say, "Hi Jason, this is Michael Wall. Nick gave me your number. Listen, I understand that NFC let you go, but I want you to come work for Wall Enterprises and be the President and Chairman of our US Division. Don't worry about the money. We will make that work. I need you to come as soon as you can. We will get the deal done. Bye, Jason—let's talk soon."

Jason exclaimed, "Are you serious? Shaunny, that was Michael Wall! That is incredible!"

"I know it's Michael Wall. Now I want my WallLand annual pass—for life! But seriously, there are more," Shaunny replied. She began to play the next message.

"Hi Jason, this is Paul. Paul Norman. Listen, I have several companies calling me and asking whether I know you. I did get a personal call from Michael Wall. I also got a call from the board chair of 365 Fitness. They know you are on the market. Please call me at your earliest convenience."

Jason could not believe what he was hearing. "What! I was going nowhere with them before. And now . . . what's this all about?"

"It's God, Jason. I know it. But wait, there is one more."

"Hi Jason, this is Jon Brames. We exchanged e-mails about a month ago, and I want to fly you out to our offices. I think there is something to what you were saying . . . and maybe this is or is not the time . . . but we should talk more."

"Shaunny, are you serious? This is coming out of—" And then he caught himself. "Okay, Shaunny, this has to be God. I had nothing lined up, and then after a week . . . okay I will see you at the house soon. I'm pulling up. I love you."

Jason pulled up into the driveway and saw his new home in a different light. *This isn't for us. It's for others. With whatever God gives me, it's for others, not me,* he thought.

He grabbed his bags, walked in the door, and gazed upon his beautiful wife. She threw her arms around him and said, "I'm so proud of you, Jason!"

Jason held her tightly and kissed her for a long, long moment. He pulled back to see a look of shock on her face and realized suddenly how his habit of short kisses and limited affection must have hurt her in the past. She'd experienced him always rushing off to the next thing—always treating potential business opportunities as more important than her. He said, "I love you, Shaunny. I'm so sorry about the way things have been. Things are going to change because I've changed. I've had an encounter with the living God who I know loves me. This is about more than leadership. This is about more than me. This is about more than us."

"Jason, I am grateful to get to spend my days here on earth with you!" Shaunny beamed.

He saw Shaunny in a different light too. He saw someone handpicked by God to be a support and helpmate to him. He looked at her with love, knowing that she had helped him get through his recent storms. He had just been too ungrateful and blind to notice it.

"So now we have two questions," said Jason. "Where do we go to dinner? And who do I call back first?"

"I think that's an easy one, Jason. Michael Wall called you first . . ."

"And you want your annual pass!" Jason joked.

They both laughed.

"I'm going to call Michael Wall, and then I'm going to fly out to see Jon Brames. Nick told me not to throw myself into my next leadership challenge, but he didn't say anything about not listening to potential offers. I think this Wall Enterprises opportunity could be something special, and they need someone like me. But the work that Jon Brames does, that could easily be for the future," Jason said. He could feel the tension between the desire to jump in with both feet and the desire to listen to Nick's warnings.

"I have Michael Wall's number right here, honey," said Shaunny, showing Jason the number.

Jason picked up the phone and dialed Michael.

"Michael Wall here."

Jason was shocked. He thought he was going to get Michael's assistant.

"Wow, Michael. It's good to talk to you. Thank you very much for the message," Jason said.

"I need you to come see me," Michael replied. "I will send out my helicopter, so there's no need to drive. Go to the Bales Airport tomorrow, and meet the helicopter there at 3:00 p.m. Do you have a family?"

"Thanks, Michael. I am very much impressed. Yes, my wife Shaunny is right here with me."

"I will fly you both out for the weekend. You can stay at our suite at the Wall Hotel."

Jason turned to Shaunny. "Shaunny, are you up for a trip to WallLand?"

"Are you kidding me? Um . . . yes!"

"Mr. Wall, that's an affirmative," Jason said.

"I will see you tomorrow then," Michael replied.

"Yes, sir."

Jason hung up the phone, looked at Shaunny, and gave her another long kiss. They were as happy as school kids going on a field trip.

12

THE FLIGHT

Twenty-four hours could not pass by quickly enough. After a beautiful dinner out at one of their favorite sushi restaurants, Jason and Shaunny were as excited as they had been on their honeymoon. The possibilities seemed endless.

They drove to and arrived at the Bales Airport. They parked near Helicopter Charters, LLC. As they looked through the iron gates, they saw a black helicopter with *Wall Enterprises* labeled on it in white. The attendant in front of the gate asked for their identification, and then upon seeing it, brought them directly to the helicopter.

When they stepped onto the platform and into the helicopter, they saw individual tan leather seats with double harnesses. They also saw a middle-aged man with aviator glasses on.

"Welcome aboard, Mr. and Mrs. Irving. I'm James Manahan. I will be your pilot for today," he said. "We have a short flight to the Wall Hotel. Please put on the ear protectors there by your seats, make yourselves comfortable, and enjoy the ride."

After the pilot provided a few more basic instructions on procedure, he touched several switches and they heard the swirling sound of the propeller. He then pushed down on the helicopter flight controls. The helicopter lifted slowly off the ground. They were in the air. As the helicopter gained altitude, Jason saw the city with new eyes. He saw the way that the roads, mountains, and city were designed. He saw the landscape in front of him. He saw it as he had never seen it before. Within fifteen minutes they were approaching a sprawling set of buildings, roller coasters, and a large sign. It was WallLand.

"This is the best trip ever!" Shaunny exclaimed to Jason. "I get to go to WallLand, and there's no traffic!"

Jason laughed. The helicopter began approaching the top of a building on the right. As Jason looked down, he saw a circular yellow pattern on the building's roof. They were coming down on top of it. They slowly approached, and a man with two red glowsticks began to wave the pilot in. They were now heading straight down at a slower speed. Jason then felt the slight impact of the helicopter's rails on the pad below. They had touched down.

Jason heard the swishing of the propeller begin to slow down, until it came to a stop.

"Mr. and Mrs. Irving. We have touched down," the pilot said.

They were met by two young men dressed in yellow and black checkered uniforms, with yellow hats, who opened the door.

"Welcome to Wall Hotel," said one.

"May I have your bags, sir?" said the other.

"Yes, of course," Jason said, handing him their bags.

He is rolling out the red carpet. This is it, Jason thought.

They were then escorted into the hotel. As they walked in, Jason noticed the intricate patterns on the walls, the antique chandeliers, and the marquetry on the mahogany hardwood floors. They took a secure elevator one floor down from the roof to a level labeled "PH." When they exited the elevator, they saw various paintings in the hallways: one was an abstract composed of thick brushstrokes in bright colors on the canvas; another was a painting of the city in black and white with WallLand prominently lit in color. There were also floor-to-ceiling windows by the elevator, overlooking the city. The men then stopped outside Room One. They opened the double doors.

As Jason and Shaunny walked in, they saw that it was an entire loft with floor-to-ceiling views of the city. There was a large fireplace, an eighty-two-inch flat-screen television, four different bedrooms, and a large bathroom.

There was a chilled bottle of champagne waiting in the living room, with a note attached. It read:

> Mr. and Mrs. Irving:
>   Welcome to Wall Hotel. Mr. Irving, after you have settled in, please meet Mr. Wall in the private conference room down the hall.
>   Sincerely yours,
>   Kirk Nipolante
>   General Manager, Wall Hotel

Jason turned to Shaunny, who was admiring the space, and said, "Okay, love, why don't you get all settled in. I'm going to meet with Michael."

Jason looked into the mirror next to the bar area, checking his blue, slimline suit, which he wore with a white, crisp shirt and a black tie. He adjusted his tie and checked the mirror to ensure it was perfectly centered.

Shaunny exclaimed, "Don't you look handsome! You got this, babe!"

"I love you," Jason said.

Jason walked out, closing the doors behind him. He walked to the conference room. The men in the yellow suits stood outside of it.

"Welcome, Mr. Irving. Please come in," one man said.

As Jason walked in, he saw Michael sitting on a black leather couch, sipping on a coffee. There were bright, clear views of the city behind him.

"Jason, good to see you again," Michael said as he rose from the couch, welcoming him.

"Michael, I can't believe I'm here," Jason replied. "I'm taking in the moment."

"Believe it. Now did you get here all right?"

"No problems. I think I could get used to this," Jason replied.

"I think you will adjust to it. Now, Jason, let's sit down and talk business. Come, sit."

Jason took a seat opposite Michael in a black leather chair.

"Can I get you anything? Billy here will take care of you," Michael said.

"Thank you. How about an Arnold Palmer?"

"Certainly," Billy said.

Michael continued, "Not two days from when we met last week, our Chairman of our US Division decided to retire. Normally, we promote strictly from within for culture reasons. But this situation is unique because it is time, in my estimation, for a shakeup. I need someone to come in with a different perspective, someone who has been through and can handle the fire of leadership. And I think that is you."

Jason was honored. But he also was ready to be honest.

"Michael, I have tremendous respect for you, and I would not be here if I did not take this seriously. But my main concern, and what I want to reflect on, is whether I am ready for leadership. Nick advised me to not jump on the next opportunity. He was very specific about this. He advised me to take stock of my leadership. And I think that I need some more time, and I want to make sure that Shaunny and I are going to be okay. I have not been the best husband as of late," Jason said.

"Oh, I understand, believe me," Michael reassured him. "This position will take everything you have, but I will not tolerate that coming at the expense of the leader's family. We force vacations, we encourage people to leave for important family events, and we won't tolerate unhealthy marriages. You will lead out of the health of your marriage. I think what you will find is that there are two to three crises every year, and those times come unexpectedly. You are needed and expected to handle and lead during those times, but we will be prepared. We will have strategized. You will have resources at your disposal—analysts, information, support staff, and leadership staff. The access you will have will be unlike any other place, I am sure. I will resource you, but I will need your leadership. With James's retirement, we need someone in the position right away, and I'd like to keep James on as a consultant during the transition."

Jason could have pinched himself. He was about to have more access than he had ever had to information, to research, and to people. This was a great responsibility, though, and it would take great courage for him to respond. He wondered whether this was his call and his time.

"Sir, your Arnold Palmer," Billy said, holding out the drink tray.

"Thank you, Billy," Jason said, taking the glass and beginning to take a sip.

Michael then added matter-of-factly as he handed Jason a folded note, "Oh, and compensation starts at the number here, with stock options. How does that sound to you?"

Jason opened the note and almost choked. He could not believe what he was reading. He would be making more every two weeks than he often made all year. *Is this really happening?* he wondered.

He attempted to tone down his excitement and, with effort, said evenly, "This is certainly an exhilarating offer. I will have to run this by Shaunny though."

"I encourage you to do so and would expect nothing less," Michael said.

With that, Michael and Jason discussed some other details—where he would work, what the expectations were, and whether their visions were aligned.

After they had hashed everything out, Jason shook Michael's hand and returned to the suite where his wife was waiting.

"Shaunny," he said, as he came into the suite's living room, "you won't believe this. The Chairman of Wall Enterprises for the US division position, it's real. And the compensation package is unreal!"

"Wow! Jason. That is . . . amazing!" Shaunny appeared dumbfounded.

"The one thing I am thinking about is whether this is our next step and how this would affect our relationship," Jason said.

"Thank you for thinking of me, Jason. I love you. I am overwhelmed by the goodness of God in my life that he would allow me to be with a man like you. Of course I support you! We will make this work."

"I also want to . . . to pray about this. I want to give it a night before accepting anything. Will you pray with me?" Jason said.

Shaunny was silent. She seemed to be stunned. He knew she had never heard him pray.

Jason began, "God, I know that you are behind all of this. And I am thankful for that. As much as the salary and great things that come with this position are tempting, I want what you want for my life. I want my will and your will to be the same. I give this decision to you, and I pray that you would lead us and guide us. I pray that you make this decision clear for us."

Then Jason said, "Shaunny, I think I have some clarity." After praying, he knew what he had to do.

He had to talk with Bill Benton about it.

13

A New Beginning

The next day Jason woke up and turned to Shaunny, looking for a sign of confirmation of the decision. Part of him did not want to talk with Bill, but the other part of him knew that this was what was next.

Shaunny was just waking up. Sleepily, she said, "Babe, I'll tell you what's in my heart for you. When you sought out good advice from Nick, it was life-changing. Seek out good advice again. Talk to Bill."

Jason admitted, "Part of me doesn't want to call him. But there's a part of me that knows it's the right thing to do."

Jason prayed, "God, help me on this call with Bill. I want your will, not mine."

He looked at his phone, charging by the nightstand. He reached over and picked it up, then got out of bed and stood in his pajamas. "Okay, here we go."

He dialed Bill.

He heard Bill's voice on the other line. "Jason, is that you? How are you?"

"Great, actually, Bill. Never been better. Getting fired was the best thing that could have happened to me. So much has happened since then. I'm calling because I need your advice. I'm wondering whether I should take a position I was offered."

"What position?" Bill asked.

"Chairman of Wall Enterprises, US."

"That's a big role, Jason. Lot of responsibility. Tell me about your time with Nick."

"At first, I have to admit I was angry. And I wanted to prove you wrong. But then as I went through the leadership challenges, I began to change. And I realized that I had been doing leadership on my own. God wasn't in any part of it. And now I realize that I need him, and I don't want to get ahead of myself. I don't want to become a leadership casualty. No amount of money is worth that," Jason responded.

"Jason, I'm glad you came to me and glad that you have been able to put your past at NFC behind you. If you were going to a solely high-performance environment in your next position, the pressure would be too tempting, and the cracks in your leadership would break you apart. But with Michael . . . he is even more intense than me, but he will support and empower you to become a better leader than I could ever dream. And he has been through all the leadership challenges himself. So, I think here in your next move you need to be clear about what's important to you and see if that fits within the structure of what they need. That way you serve both Wall Enterprises and continue to serve your family. And I think your time with Nick has awakened you to the unhealthy side of leadership, a side that I saw in you. I was not going to let that happen again to someone under my watch. Once that type of leadership comes off the rails, nothing is enough—no amount of growth, power, money—it simply cannot fill your soul."

There was a pause, and then Bill said, "One more thing . . . I hope you can forgive me for letting you go."

"Thanks, Bill. I know it's the only way you could get through to me," Jason replied.

Bill continued, "And know that I was getting calls about you from other leaders, and I felt it was my responsibility to do something drastic because once you received the offers, you would not have the fire lit under you to want to make the change. That is how it often happens in a transition. God will leave you with no other options than to lean on him so that you will submit to his process of transformation. Only then will you be ready for the next assignment. And what I hear on the other line, Jason, is a man who appears ready, but you will need to experience this for yourself."

"Bill, you don't know how much that means to me. I will forever be grateful for you," Jason said.

"I'm just glad it's working out. Now go accept the offer before he retracts it!"

"Yes, sir!" Jason replied with excitement and hung up the phone.

"This is your time, Jason. Seize it!" Shaunny encouraged him.

"So you are in this with me?"

"Yes. I love you," Shaunny said.

Jason then called Michael from his cell phone.

Michael answered. "Yes, Jason?"

"Michael, now I'm ready. I certainly wasn't before. But now I'm ready."

"I will have my assistant draw up the paperwork. Get some rest and enjoy the remainder of the weekend with Shaunny on me. You are going to need it."

"Thanks, Michael. My soul has found its rest in God. And I will make sure I am ready to be a servant, visionary, coachable, courageous, and transformed leader for you and Wall Enterprises."

"Spoken like a true Nick Savant follower."

"I follow Nick as he follows Christ."

"Amen, Jason. Amen."

14

So Much for the Honeymoon

Jason woke up much earlier than normal. It was four o'clock in the morning. He found his old Bible his mom had bought him years ago. He dusted it off and flipped through it, then slowly started journaling and praying.

It was a new and unusual practice for him.

He prayed, "God, I know you are there. If I'm honest, I know there has been change, but I am not fully convinced of it myself. I need your help today. I pray that rather than serve myself, you would give me a heart to serve and love others. I know that I have limited vision because of my selfishness. I pray that you would give me vision and imagination for what could be, for the sake of our leaders, our employees, and our customers. I know that in my own strength and pride, I want to do things my way. Help me stay open and teachable, help me to be coachable today, to learn new things.

"I am afraid. When I am on my own, I am afraid, and I know that is when I do not believe that you are with me. I pray that you would go with me and before me today and that with you I would fear nothing. I pray for courage today. And I'm not one that wants to change easily, but I submit myself to you and I pray that you would transform me into a leader that can meet the circumstances, problems, and situations I will face today. I pray that when I fall, you would pick me back up again. I pray that your Holy Spirit would go with me today. I know that I can't do this without you. Amen."

It was five o'clock in the morning. Jason put on his new suit that Shaunny had helped him pick out. He gave her a kiss, another long one, and drove out to WallLand for his first day.

He came early to spend time greeting and getting to know people—janitors, front desk staff, secretaries, assistants, and VPs. He made a list of names for himself. He then took the elevator floor up to his office, with a 180-degree view of WallLand, just down the hall from Michael Wall himself.

Michael knocked on his open door. "Jason, you are going to have training, lots of it, but we have an emergency, and I want your input on this. Can you come over?"

So much for the honeymoon, Jason thought. *I came in early to get settled, and I'm being drawn into an emergency meeting.*

He walked into Michael's office not knowing what to expect. He saw a virtual boardroom on the screen, with leaders from all over the world. Here in person included James Jesshum, the current Chairman of the US division who was stepping down and retiring. He was a grizzled veteran of the company, with a raspy and authoritative voice.

Though James had retired, he was hoping to place his COO in the position, and he did not appreciate that Michael Wall had stepped in and upset his arrangements. James was a loyal Wall-Land employee who had been there since day three—forty years ago. He was a straight shooter who did not pull punches. Early on, he was Michael's hatchet man who would take on the tough projects.

"Team," Michael said, "I would like to formally introduce you to Jason Irving, who will be our new Chairman in the US. I informed him that we are breaking protocol for his training because of this emergency meeting. Jason, let me bring you up to speed. James is set to retire in three months, but we have found a replacement faster than we anticipated, and the Board confirmed your acceptance ahead of other candidates, including Kelly Manchester, his planned successor. Then a wrench was thrown in the plans. James is threatening to quit in the next week if Kelly is not the successor. He says that he is looking out for the best interests of WallLand, and I believe he is sincere in that belief. James is accelerating his retirement and has indicated that Kelly will leave and has other offers on the table. He is telling me that Kelly has been running day-to-day operations for years, so that without her, you will be walking into a sinkhole."

James interjected, "Michael, I will add this—I realize that you are starry-eyed with Jason Irving—and by the way, Jason, I'm not going to say it's nice to meet you, because you are not welcome here—but Michael, you're making the wrong move. And Jason, I want you to know that I asked for you to be present so that you would know what you are dealing with. I don't backstab. You will always know where you stand with me."

Jason, feeling the insecurity and fear inside, also sensed courage rising up within him.

"Michael, may I speak for a moment?" Jason asked.

"Yes, please go right ahead."

"James, it *is* a pleasure to meet you. Let me make sure I understand what you are saying. You have groomed someone for this position, Kelly Manchester, the current COO to be specific, and without Kelly, the division will lose her institutional knowledge, experience, and having another person in the role would cause harm to the division. Do I have that right?" Jason asked.

"That's fair. I would not say cause harm. Rather, that it's not in keeping with our culture of hiring from within, and I don't think you have what it takes to be successful here." James responded.

That stung, Jason thought. *Did he really just say that? What am I doing here? I can't believe I thought that I would be able to do this.*

"James, I respect that you are speaking your mind to me rather than behind me. And I believe you want what's best for WallLand. I do not presume to have your knowledge. But the decision was made by the Board and by Michael Wall, who, I assume, are fully aware of all the factors involved, including the potential departure of Kelly Manchester. That said, I would like to meet with you, with Kelly, and the team, and if I determine that your assessment is in fact the case, that I would be doing a disservice by staying in this role, I would be happy to report these findings to Michael and the Board. I have no self-serving agenda in mind. Yet, I do not want us to needlessly extend this. I propose we reconvene in forty-eight hours. Does that sound fair?"

Jason could not believe what was coming out of his mouth. James came in firing, and he'd managed to not simply fire back, but to diffuse the situation and move the company forward. He was listening; he was acting with courage.

"James," Michael said, "that sounds like a very reasonable proposal. Do you agree to postpone the decision to your resignation?"

"Yes," James acquiesced. "But, Jason, I want to see you right now." James seemed like he was seething inside, still attempting to assert control.

"I am happy to meet with you. I am sure you can understand that I need at least another thirty minutes to get situated. How about we meet at eight-thirty?" Jason wanted a little more time.

"That's fine," James said, "but come to my office."

"Agreed," Jason said.

Michael gathered the attention of the room and screens, "Ladies and gentlemen, let's reconvene in forty-eight hours. Jason, I give you full authority for the next two days to resolve this. If you can't, we will rescind your contract." The room became silent.

Jason was taken aback by the comments, but responded, "Michael, I would like a few minutes with you."

Michael then walked with Jason back into his office.

"Michael, that was a great way to start the first day," Jason said, joking.

"I am glad you find it humorous. I have no choice but to rescind your contract if these are the facts, as James has stated," Michael responded.

"I'm not worried about that right now, Michael, but thank you. What I need is some coaching on James. Can you give me any insight into him?"

"Jason, I do not get too involved in these decisions. I set up the rules, and I let the cream rise to the top. I like to know that I have leaders that can fight their way through battles. What I can tell you is that James will do everything to keep Kelly in that role. Most people are intimidated by him. If you let yourself get intimidated, you will lose. I want to see if you can figure this out."

It seemed to Jason that Michael was trying to call out the leader within him. "Thanks, Michael," Jason said. "That is helpful, but I really do want to learn here. I have a plan."

After Michael left, Jason shut the door and began looking through something he read earlier in the day. In Deuteronomy, God urged the Jewish people not to fight until God had delivered their enemies into their hands, even enemies stronger than them. *The Lord is fighting for me,* Jason thought. He began to pray to God for direction before heading into battle. He felt like he heard God saying, *Learn what James and Kelly's arguments are. Don't attempt to pulverize them, or to conquer them in your own strength. Learn what they are saying. Learn why they are saying it.*

The truth was that Jason was intimidated, but he was walking ahead with courage.

Then the phone rang and Jason answered, hearing the voice of a composed woman on the other line, "Jason, this is James Jesshum's office. James is expecting you in five minutes."

"I will be right there, thank you."

Jason walked across the hall, and by the looks of the faces of the assistants, word of the conflict had gotten around. People were watching him, like watching a young up-and-coming fighter approaching a prize champion, expecting the head of the young fighter to return bloodied and bruised.

"Jason, get in here," James said. Jason felt like he was walking into the belly of the beast. The sign above his office might as well have read, "Abandon all hope, ye who enter here."

15

THE FIGHT

"Listen, let's cut the crap," said James heatedly. "You have no business being here. I know you were fired from NFC before this. I know you have been with Nick Savant. Don't try to pull any of that Nick Savant stuff on me. None of those leadership gimmicks are going to work here."

"James, I am here to listen, and I have no gimmicks," Jason said calmly. "Nick Savant is a great man, but you need not believe in his methods. Please tell me more about what is going to happen to this division if I remain here, you retire, and Kelly leaves."

"Jason, listening is not going to help you. You failed before, and you are going to fail again."

"James, there is a chance I could fail, but my heart is to truly know what is happening, and I have a mandate to fulfill within the next forty-eight hours. So are you going to help me or not?" Jason was done playing games.

"Okay," James said, resigned. "Here: read this." James handed Jason a two hundred-page report.

Jason looked at the thick stack of papers and shook his head. "This is going to take me two days just to read and digest. If that is how you are going to play it, we can play this game. Tell me what your conclusions are. I am going to include those in my report. So it's in your best interest to explain the conclusions to me."

"Fine. Kelly has been at WallLand for twenty-six years. She has been my COO for six years. She has been effectively running the company for the last two years, and I have been grooming her to be chairman. Without her, this division cannot run. You are simply not going to be able to keep up without her. We are both on our way out if you stay. Neither of us believe in Nick Savant's ways or that they are a good fit for WallLand. Anyone could have advised Michael Wall in the early years. Nick was lucky, and his luck is running out. The company needs to change, and Nick Savant is in the way. It's either innovate or die."

"Thanks, James. I think I have heard what I needed to hear. I'd like to speak with Kelly."

"Cindy!" James raised his voice, and his receptionist came running at his call. "I need you to bring Kelly here right away," James told her, and then he turned to Jason. "She will be on her way."

Kelly Manchester walked in a few moments later. She was wearing a crisp pinstripe suit with red heels.

"So this is Jason," Kelly said to James. She took a seat across from Jason, next to James.

"Yes, this is me," Jason said.

"I don't know how you are not depressed. Didn't you just get fired from NFC? I have no idea who you have been brown-nosing to end up at Wall Enterprises," Kelly said with anger.

"Kelly, listen, I understand that I am not welcome, to either of you. Help me understand what's happening in this division. As I told the Board today, if what I hear leads me to believe that it's not good for business, I will gladly submit my resignation," Jason said.

"Jason, the fact is that though I have been reporting to the chairman, I have been running the division and preparing for James's retirement. Nobody knows this place better than me. I have over twenty-five years of history and experience here, and I'm simply not going to be passed over again, and this time from the outside. It's either up or out, in my opinion. So I will be out if you stay."

"Understood, Kelly," Jason responded. Then he said, "Tell me about what is going to be the most difficult for me when I step into this role."

"Well, you are under constant pressure to make numbers, you have to deal with endless expectations, you will get no sleep and never see your family again. But you will get bonused. I was like you once, bright-eyed and eager to see things change, but then I resigned myself to the fact that I could not change *this*." Her gesture took in the entire office. "It was too big of a ship. That's why I need control. That's the only way things can change. I would do 80 percent of things differently than how they are done here now—if it was up to me."

Jason had heard all he needed to hear. He had a plan.

"Thank you both," Jason said. "I appreciate your candor."

Though Jason had courageously walked into the meeting and felt ready to report to Michael, something about it seemed too easy. His instinct told him something was being held back. There was more he needed to learn.

He headed back to his office and called a meeting with the rest of the executive team from his division of Wall Enterprises.

Within fifteen minutes, Chief Marketing Officer Gerald Cheng, Chief Financial Officer Bob Marquist, and Chief Innovation Officer Josina Riddick were present in his office.

Jason opened by saying, "Thank you all for coming on such short notice. As I am sure you are aware, James is set to retire, and Kelly was the successor-in-waiting. I am here to see what other information I need to know. We will have a group leadership meeting now. I am trying to determine what will happen if Kelly leaves the division."

Bob spoke up first. "I've been with the company for thirty-one years," he said. "To tell the truth, I'm getting ready to retire and enjoy my golden years with my family. But WallLand matters to me. It's been part of my life since I was young." He paused, rubbed his chin, and then added, "All of that to say, Jason, I'm glad that we are meeting here. I'm looking forward to getting to know you more. But if we lose Kelly, I estimate we would have a 17 percent decrease in revenue year one. Then we would need to restructure the division, make cuts, and likely lay off about one thousand people."

"Thanks, Bob," Jason said. "Why the 17 percent decrease and layoff of one thousand people?"

"Kelly is integral to the culture of this division. She drives our initiatives. She is the number one person for this role, and there are not any replacements. It would take a year to learn this stuff," Bob said.

"Okay, anyone else?" Jason kept his demeanor composed, but he felt nervous.

Gerald spoke up. "Kelly is a marketing genius. She has been instrumental in our branding and messaging, and we are in the middle of revamping that process, which she has allowed me to lead. Without that initiative and her direction, we will miss our deadlines and the revenue targets that track with them."

Josina added, "Jason, I appreciate that you are listening. The key with Kelly is that she knows how everything is supposed to run. Yes, we have operations manuals and protocols, but she has institutional knowledge that will ruin this division if she leaves with it."

"Who is her successor?" Jason asked. "If she was to be chairman, who was going to be the COO?"

"You," Josina said.

"What?" Jason asked, shocked.

"You were going to be recruited to the COO position. And then when you were fired, we were sure you would be available. Only then did we find out that you would be coming in as the chairman. Frankly, none of us want you as the chairman. We are doing well. You should be the COO, not the chairman. This is Kelly's ship, and we all want to work for her."

Jason now knew what James and Kelly had up their sleeve. His entire leadership team was going to sabotage him as the chairman. Now Jason had to figure out the bigger vision of how it all fit together.

"Please tell me," Jason said, "What do each of you want?"

"Stability," Bob said.

"Control over this new initiative," Gerald said.

"A culture of innovation," Josina said.

"Those are all good things," Jason said. "But we need to be part of a vision bigger than that. Now, rather than tell me what you each want, tell me in one word what you each contribute to the team."

"One word?" Josina asked. "That's an idea—difficult to sum up though."

"I know. It's not easy. But tell me one word. Who wants to start?" Jason asked.

Josina went first, "Innovation. Innovation brings people together, gathers their ideas, and makes the culture what it is. Without innovation, we have no culture."

"That's good, that's very good! What about everyone else?" Jason asked.

"I'll go," Gerald said. "Messaging. How we market to our consumer is how we message and connect with them intimately. That also is how we understand ourselves internally."

"Perfect, Gerald! I love that. Messaging is extremely important. Bob, what about you?" Jason asked.

"Process. I run the numbers to see if the gross margins make sense. Every idea comes through the financial process."

"Great, everyone! I love this team already. Now, tell me, what one word comes to mind for Kelly and James. What do they bring?"

"Direction. James is phenomenal at setting a direction," Gerald said.

"Systems," said Bob. "Kelly systematizes everything we have done, and she does it well. And now she has been taking on the direction component, doing both very well. I'm afraid of what will happen without her."

"Team, thank you for being honest. What I see here is that we need direction and systems. I can setup the systems, but that is not my strongest suit. What we need is to find the strongest person for that system role, and the strongest person for the role of direction. That is the best way that I can serve this team right now. Is there anything else you want to add?"

"Not now," Josina said.

Jason nodded, then looked around, but no one else spoke up. "Okay. I think I'm ready to speak with Michael."

Jason shook everyone's hand. He now knew what was happening. Josina was the leader among the rest of the group, and everyone's personal interests were driving the desire to avoid change. He knew he had to meet with Michael next.

He walked out and went straight into Michael's office.

"Michael, do you have a minute?" Jason asked.

"Not really, but I will make one for you. Jason, I'm terribly sorry that training has not gone on as usual . . . this is not like Wall Enterprises one bit. But truth be told I am getting too old for these battles. It's good to have someone around who can fight them as well."

Me? He might think I'm a fighter, Jason thought, *but I can't get ahead of myself. This needs to be handled the right way.*

"I don't have the final answer, but please tell me what you think. James has been grooming Kelly, and it is a matter of legacy for him. He wanted to leave a legacy at Wall Enterprises, and if Kelly doesn't get the role, he will think his work here is somehow incomplete. Kelly has been groomed as and has acted as the successor. James is phenomenal with the direction that the team needed, and Kelly has been excellent with systems. Now Kelly thinks she is ready to lead, but I see things in her that remind me of myself as I was just a short time ago. James is concerned with his legacy. With your permission, I'd like to work on a proposal and setup a meeting with you, James, and Kelly."

"Of course, Jason. I am releasing you to do whatever you need to do. I will call the meeting for four in the afternoon today. Does that sound good?"

"Excellent," Jason replied.

Jason hurried back to his office. His old instinct would have been to begin work right away on the new project. Instead he closed the door, sat in his chair overlooking WallLand, and began to reflect on the day. *This has been a momentous day, but the battle is not done yet. If James retires early and Kelly quits, this division will be in trouble, and I will be out of a job. Michael's hand will be forced.*

He then prayed, "God, I know you are here with me. I am not sure what to do right now. Thank you for bringing me this far. But I'm not sure what to do next. I pray for clear direction from you, and I surrender this position to you. I pray that you would change the hearts of James and Kelly. I pray that love, rather than pride and defensiveness, would come from my heart. I pray that you would soften them. I pray that you would fight my battle for me. I will wait for you."

He paused in the silence. And then Jason opened his Bible. It landed on Psalm 75, which read, "It is God who executes judgment, putting down one and lifting up another."[5] He thought about that verse a bit. Then he opened his Bible again, and he landed on James 4. It read, "God opposes the proud but gives grace to the humble."[6]

Jason thought about the pride in him that wanted to use power and authority to make things happen. But he knew that he was here to be a servant. He was not here to build his own kingdom, nor to lift himself up.

Yet, he was still nervous and afraid of being humiliated in today's upcoming meeting. He couldn't help but remember that the last time he had been called into a meeting, he'd walked into it confidently expecting a promotion . . . and walked out of it as a man who had just been fired.

16

THE KEYS ON THE BATTLEFIELD

It all led to this. It was 3:45 p.m., fifteen minutes before the meeting. Jason was sitting in silence at his desk, gazing at the keychain he had just earned last week. He reminded himself of each lesson. *Servant leadership. Let the vision come to you. Be coachable. Find courage to face failure. Leaders need to be challenged so they can be transformed.* He was praying for wisdom and strength for the meeting. He still did not have the full strategy, but he was believing in faith that God would intervene.

He then heard a buzz, and a voice through the intercom said, "Mr. Irving, Michael is ready for you now."

"Thank you. I will be right there," Jason said.

After hanging up, he turned his heart once more to God. "Be with me," he prayed. "I need your help."

Then Jason walked out of his office and into Michael's office.

He walked right into tension that could be cut with a knife. James and Kelly were present, sitting defiantly side-by-side.

Michael said, "Now, let's go ahead and begin. James and Kelly, you have the floor first."

"Thank you, Michael." James stood up and walked right up to Jason, six inches from his face. It was intimidating. "Jason, the reality is that if you stay, I am going to retire and Kelly is going to leave to work for a company that appreciates her. And there is nothing that you can do to stop this. Nothing! Except leaving. You need to go. That's what's best for Wall Enterprises. I'm not sure what Nick taught you over at his palace of mystery, but that's the reality."

Jason took a step back for some breathing room and responded, "James, you have complete freedom to retire. And Kelly, should you choose to leave, you may. I do not dispute that. But let me ask you—James, what legacy are you going to leave by provoking Kelly's departure?"

James looked angrily at Jason, "Very simple: she will go on to be a CEO of another company that appreciates what I have invested in her. She is not going to work for NFC's leftovers."

Jason took that shot in the gut. He remembered Nick hitting him there last week. He sensed his pride wanting to retaliate for James bruising his ego and self-interest.

But he knew now where he was and where he stood. From that place of stability, Jason responded, "Being let go from NFC was the best thing that could have happened to my leadership. I was on a path to destruction." He then turned to Kelly. "Kelly, let me ask you, how is your family life and your health right now?"

James interrupted, "You don't need to answer that."

"That's neither your concern, nor your business, Jason," Kelly responded.

Jason said confidently, "I have been the over-dedicated leader who let my family life suffer, and I am not going to have leaders under me suffer that same fate. Business matters, but family matters much more. Kelly, we need to go in a different direction. There are some things I am seeing in your leadership that concern me. Also, there are two types of leaders in this world. Drivers . . . and coaches. Drivers push results, and coaches . . . well you can count on them to develop leaders. You've done an excellent job turning things around, but Wall Enterprises is going to need a different kind of leader—a leader with a coaching mentality—for what we are doing next. I'm proposing to Michael that we bring in a leader from another region with a knack for systems and a coaching mentality to take over for you and become COO. I'm sorry."

Jason then turned to James, "And James, your legacy is up to you. If you want to leave, you can. If you want to stay on as a consultant, I'd like to learn from you. But if not, we can have your retirement party this week. That is up to you."

Kelly and James looked stunned. Jason could see they hadn't expected the leverage they thought they held to just suddenly lose all its power. Even Jason was surprised at the words that came out of his own mouth.

Jason added, "And, of course, Michael, this is subject to the approval of you and the Board."

Michael paused for a moment. He then responded, "Jason, this is what I was hoping you would do, but I needed to see this from you to be sure I'd made the right choice in hiring you. But now I'm confident you are the right man for the job."

James backed off and took a seat. "I will need to think about my future here. But I will say this: firing Kelly is a foolish move. The next time you hear from her, it will be a demand letter from her attorney!"

"Fair enough," Jason responded. "As I said, I'd like you on the journey. Please let me know by the end of the week so that we can decide either way. And Kelly, should you desire to hire an attorney, that is up to you. But based on your employment contract that I've reviewed, we can fulfill our obligations to you by paying you what's remaining on your contract, as well as paying out the weeks of vacation you haven't taken. We won't leave you empty-handed."

After hearing him out in stony silence, James and Kelly stormed out of the office, and Jason quietly stood by. He stood in his own transformation as a leader. He was a different person. He was not the same man by any means.

Michael came around from behind his desk to put his hand on Jason's shoulder. "Jason, I know you have what it takes. I have never seen anyone handle James and Kelly the way you just did. It reminded me of . . . well . . . Nick."

Jason shook his head. "I'm a different man. I can't take the credit for it. This was God's work. I sensed his presence with me this entire time."

"I believe that. And, Jason, from what I've just seen, I think it's clear that you've internalized all the lessons Nick had to teach you."

"Thank you," said Jason, absently. He couldn't help it: he was still thinking about Kelly, her destructive drive, and her anger. She reminded him so much of himself. As he turned to go, Jason placed his hand in his pocket and felt the cool metal of the keys of leadership brushing against his fingers. Jason had a flash of insight. It was sudden enough and striking enough that he just stood there for a moment, stunned.

He didn't even realize he'd paused until Michael cleared his throat and said, "Jason . . . are you okay?"

Jason shook his head. "Yes . . . sorry. Everything is okay. But I just realized that there's one more thing I learned from Nick that I haven't put into practice yet."

Michael raised his eyebrow inquiringly.

"It's not something Nick ever said officially . . . but it appears to me that once a leader has made it through The Gauntlet, there is only one way to keep the five keys of leadership."

Michael smiled, as if he knew what was coming. "And what's that, Jason?"

Jason could feel himself smiling, as well as sense the tears welling up in his eyes. "The only way you ever keep anything that's really important: you give it away. And for the first time in a long time, I have something to give."

Michael laughed. "Oh yes," he said, "Without question that is at the heart of Nick's message . . . and I think you've *definitely* grabbed a hold of it!"

Jason laughed and wiped the tears from his eyes. "Well, then, if you will excuse me for a moment. I need to give Kelly a certain number."

And as he walked out of Michael's office, he walked with the firm stride of a man who knew where he was going and what he was going to do next.

Pass it on, he thought. *Just like Bill did for me.*

ENDNOTES

1. Matthew 5: 3, 5, 8 MSG.

2. Isaiah 40:31a ESV.

3. Psalm 138:3 ESV.

4. Galatians 2:20 ESV.

5. Psalm 75:7 ESV.

6. James 4:6b ESV.

THE FIVE KEYS OF LEADERSHIP:
AN AFTERWORD

As I'm writing this to you, I'm looking outside the window of a plane flying above the Pacific coast towards Alaska. This vantage point offers a view of something that is difficult to perceive from the ground: the true shape of the land. With that said, I'm going to metaphorically take you on a short flight over the terrain we have covered on the ground, so that you may see it from an aerial view. My hope is that this view will help you see how the puzzle fits together for where you are right now in your leadership. Come along with me: let's look at the five keys from up here.

SERVICE

Servant leadership. When you focus on serving the needs of other people, you forget about yourself. Leadership is primarily not about self; it is primarily about others.

Therefore, the first key of leadership is service. As a leader, you have been appointed to serve other people. Nick said to Jason, "The first thing I check when I'm doing a leadership assessment is who the leader is serving: himself or others. The truth is I have done both and I have had both types of leaders over me. I began to thrive when I had someone over me serving me, and I bet you have too. That is the first key. The only type of leadership is servant leadership."

Service is where leadership begins. You may be called to serve in business, at a nonprofit, in sports, in the church, in your job, in government. It begins with whatever small task you are entrusted with. And the *telos* (or purpose) of this task is to serve another person.

Organizations begin to die when they become focused on their own survival, so it is important to remain focused on others—both those within the organization and those without.

VISION

Let the vision come to you. Vision is the second key, but it only comes with the proper application of the first key, which is service. When you begin thinking about other people and their needs, you begin to have a creative vision that encompasses more than yourself. Your vision takes in what is possible for others, for a better future. You then share the vision with such clarity that others can see it for themselves, and then your team can act on it.

Oftentimes when we are without vision for our people, we can find it by beginning to serve them in small ways. Then bigger vision for them is revealed to us—along with the steps to get there. Companies and organizations begin dying the day they turn inward, focusing on their own needs and not on those of their team and the people they serve together.

Think of vision as being able to see things clearly. If you have selfishness, bitterness, greed, and other vices gripping your heart, you are not going to be able to see clearly. But when you have a pure heart, the vision will come to you.

Vision is a picture of what the future could be, for the benefit of others. The most powerful visions are given by God for the sake of the people you lead—to help the people your team serves.

COACHABILITY

Be coachable. To become a great leader, you must take every opportunity to learn, whether from books, classes, mentors, or experience. Often failures are the greatest teachers—even if they're also the most painful.

We must face our failures and be willing to ask, "What have I learned from this?"

And to learn well requires the humility to realize that you do not have all the answers and must become an *open,* rather than a *closed* system. An open system allows for a flow of information, learning, and knowledge into your life. In contrast, a closed system creates a prideful wall which cuts you off from this inflow. Coaches in our life, whether formal or informal, can accelerate learning by making the learning process a *relational* one. This book, for example, provides one process. There are many, many others. Some coaches you may meet in person. Other coaches you meet through books and media.

COURAGE

Find courage to face failure. The fourth key of leadership is courage. Failure is going to happen over and over again, but it's your preparation and your willingness to face your fears that is the key to accessing the courage within you—the courage to enter the ring again.

For a leader, courage is primarily about facing yourself and not blaming others for any failures in your own leadership. Look at any successful leader, and you will see a pattern of success following failure. In those failures lies the key to change.

Leadership creates pressure, and this pressure brings out our fears—of failure, of what people think, of getting it wrong, or even of success. Courage is that ability to take the next step, even in the face of this multitude of fears.

TRANSFORMATION

Leaders need to be challenged so they can be transformed. You will never remain the same person as a leader. The pressures, the failures, the disappointments: these are invitations to change. Yet often leaders avoid the call to change inherent in these moments by turning to workaholism, addictions, and other unhealthy behaviors. Ultimately, God is the one who transforms, and the Holy Spirit is the mediator of transformation.

Nick, seeing Jason's clear change, said, "The last key is the key of transformation. Leaders need to be challenged so that they can be transformed. And that key comes from and belongs to God. It's nothing I can do or give you. There is nothing more powerful than a transformed leader who serves, has vision, is willing to learn, and has the courage to face failure. But it's the key of transformation that is the most important.

"Jason, whether you believe in God or not, every leader has been made in his image. That image may be corrupted, broken, or marred, but that image is still there. Now the gifts God has given us? We may choose not to use them for his purposes. I believe that true leadership is theocratic leadership, meaning that leadership is given by God for the sake of others. Leadership is from God and for the purpose of loving him and loving others. If any areas of our life are out of alignment with those purposes, there will be a leadership pathology. Many leaders are self-aggrandizing, using leadership for their own gain, power, prestige, and wealth. That's why leaders need to be transformed. They often need to be challenged into transformation. And God is the greatest coach and challenger of all. He will coach you hard. But then he will love you harder afterwards. Most of a leader's problems, failures, and challenges are disguised opportunities for transformation, but a leader needs to give himself to the process. Very few ever do, and it usually takes something large and something painful happening in their lives—like it did with you—to bring leaders to the end of their ropes."

I hope, whether you are at the end of your rope or still out there energetically returning those punches, that this book provided you with an experience and a process to help you on your journey. And while I have shared keys to unlock success in your leadership, there is a far more important and valuable key. That key is you. *You* are the key to unlocking the success of your organization.

The Five Keys of Leadership:
A Discussion Guide

As a catalyst to growth, perhaps the only thing more powerful than experience is *shared* experience. I suggest reading this book with your team, discussing and applying the keys of leadership together. I have found that slowing down the process together in a group provides for more shared insight and learning. To that end, what follows is a seven-week discussion guide.

WEEK 1: CHAPTERS 1–5

Group Questions

When you hear the word "leader," what comes to mind?

In what ways can you identify with Jason's experiences?

Was there a time in your life when you failed in your leadership? How did you respond?

What are you hoping to get out of this book?

WEEK 2: CHAPTER 6

Group Questions for the Leadership Key of Service:

When was the first time you were called to serve? What was that experience like?

Has there ever been a time in your leadership when you saw yourself becoming self-centered rather than focused on service? What happened?

What would it look like for you to serve where you are in your role right now? What would change if you made service a priority?

WEEK 3: CHAPTER 7

Group Questions for the Leadership Key of Vision:

Have you ever worked under someone who inspired you with their vision? Who was it, and what was it like?

Have you ever had a vision that came to pass? What was that experience like?

Have you ever lost vision in an area where you once had vision? What was that like?

What would it be like for you to have vision where you are right now?

WEEK 4: CHAPTER 8

Group Questions for the Leadership Key of Coachability:

Have you had any great coaches in your life? What were they like?

Is there an area of your leadership where you have stopped learning and growing?

What would it look like for you to be coachable right now where you are as a leader? Where do you think you might look for mentors or resources to coach you?

WEEK 5: CHAPTER 9

Group Questions for the Leadership Key of Courage:

Can you describe a time when you were afraid and did not do the right thing?

Can you describe a time when you were afraid and did the right thing anyway?

What leadership failure of yours stands out most in your memory? What did you learn from it?

Is there an area of your leadership where you are being called to be courageous? What would it look like for you to be courageous in that area?

WEEK 6: CHAPTER 10

Group Questions for the Leadership Key of Transformation:

Are there any areas of your leadership that you have been avoiding painful self-awareness of?

Can you relate to Jason's experience of God in these chapters? Why or why not?

What are the areas of your leadership that you are being called to change?

What would it look like for you to step into your current role as a transformed leader?

WEEK 7: CHAPTERS 11–16

Group Questions for Application:

What leadership challenge are you currently facing right now?

How are you currently dealing with it?

Which keys of leadership could apply to this situation?

What would it look like to apply those keys to this leadership challenge you are facing?